A HARVEST OF G.O.L.D.
Leather Bikers on the Prowl

First Edition

Published by The Nazca Plains Corporation
Las Vegas, Nevada
2010

ISBN: 978-1-935509-54-7

Published by

The Nazca Plains Corporation ®
4640 Paradise Rd, Suite 141
Las Vegas NV 89109-8000

PUBLISHER'S NOTE
A Harvest of G.O.L.D. is a work of fiction created wholly by *G.W. Leatherman PARKS'* imagination. All characters are fictional and any resemblance to any persons living or deceased is purely by accident. No portion of this book reflects any real person or events.

Male Cover Photo, Fleshblack
Art Director, Blake Stephens

DEDICATION

Dedicated to jim,
a worthy Leatherboy,
and all the hot
Leatherbikers
who enjoy both a
cycle and a boy
between their legs.

A HARVEST OF G.O.L.D.

Leather Bikers on the Prowl

First Edition

G.W. Leatherman PARKS

CONTENTS

LEATHER BIKERS

Carson marched to the front of the room. The room was filled with men dressed in head to toe Leathers. Tough fuckers. Cigars clenched in the corner of most of their mouths. Studded gauntlets, chains on their epaulets, shit-kicking boots. It took a strong man to lead this pack of men and Carson was the man.

He banged his Leathered fist on the table once, twice, finally three times, before bellowing, "All right, shut the fuck up!"

The room finally quieted. Some of the guys leaned against the wall, dragging on their cigars. Some propped their feet on the backs of their submissives. A few actually sat in the provided chairs.

"All right, you animals. I'm calling this meeting to order."

He called Jim, the Parliamentarian, forward to take a roll call. This was an important meeting and they all knew it. All twelve Club members were present.

Roll call complete, Carson stepped back up to the makeshift podium.

"As you know, men, spring is approaching. When Leather bears like us come out of hibernation, sniff the air, and seek out willing candidates for our pleasure."

The men hooted and yelled. The men who had brought their subs slapped them on their asses.

"For every man in the Club to have a sub at his disposal, we need seven this season." Some subs had not proven worthy of the Club, some had simply dropped out. The boys who had remained, however, were good boys and the Club had embraced them warmly. Well, after fucking their asses, pulling their tits, jamming cocks down their throats, and warming their asses with floggers, that is.

The twelve Leathermen comprised the Leather and Motorcycle Club, the Gods of Leather Discipline (G.O.L.D.). Proud of their manhood, proud of their Leathers, and proud of their brotherhood while riding.

Club membership was by invitation only. A Club member was required to wear his Leathers on a daily basis, own a motorcycle, and have a strong interest in sadomasochism. Thanks to the generosity of the Club members, the Leathermen had their own headquarters with a dungeon fully outfitted with four slings, two St. Andrew's Crosses, and three workover tables.

Carson and his partner John were the founders. Carson was President and John was Vice-President.

They had handpicked the six other men who were the charter members of the Club. Selection for other members was slow and deliberate, forming a corps of tightly-bound men who put the Club above all else.

"So, men, any suggestions where we should begin our harvest of handsome young men?"

A few crude suggestions were shouted out before Rick, a charter member, suggested a very handsome young man who worked at the local Leather shop.

His qualifications were outlined by Rick who had played with the boy on several occasions in his own dungeon. "Good candidate, submissive, sturdy, has taken my ass-whippings repeatedly without the drama you sometimes get. I can assure you his hole has been stretched- takes a fisting very well. Good cocksucker. Rides. A Kawasaki, I think."

"Well, hell, that's one strike against him," interjected Butch. The guys laughed. Most of the guys rode Harleys.

Rick continued, "Wears his Leathers well. Every time I've been in the shop, he has had ass-tight Leather on. I'd nominate him for a sub position in our Club."

"Anyone else know him?" Carson asked.

Several of the guys were familiar with him and seconded the nomination.

"Okay, good, we'll put him on the list and the Review Committee will talk to him."

The names of several other young men were put forth as candidates but by the end of the official meeting, only one other name was added to the Review Committee list.

"We're going to go on a harvest run, men," Carson declared. The Leathermen shouted their approval. A date was set for the following week.

With the most crucial business out of the way, the meeting dissolved into a play party with each of the subs escorted to one of the devices in the dungeon. It was a successful evening with young asses being plowed, mouths opened wide, and jism flowing. All twelve Club members had satisfied smiles on their faces by the end of the evening.

"Okay, Leathermen, that ends the evening's business. Ride safely," Carson concluded. The men dispersed to the outside of the Club where a row of gleaming cycles awaited the men.

Carson and John rode Harleys. They quickly mounted their cycles and rode off into the night.

The two men were anxious to get home. They had two willing boys in bondage in their dungeon. These were boys they had played with only once before and they were anxious to continue their education.

Pulling their cycles into the alley behind their house, they dismounted and entered their townhouse.

"Let's have a drink before we work over the boys," Carson suggested. They both pulled cigars from their cases and lighted up. John mixed the drinks and sat a tray in front of them.

"Do you think we should have told the Club about our initiates?" John asked.

"No, not yet. It will be our little pleasure for awhile."

John reached over and thrust his tongue in Carson's throat. The two men began groping one another and were soon rolling around on the floor. Their cocks pressing against their tight Leather. Without any spoken communication, the men assumed a sixty-nine position and were soon sucking on each other's manrod.

Cocks arched forward into each other's willing mouth. Both cocks were throbbing from the sexual fire the two felt for one another.

The two had met in high school. By the time they were seniors both had their first motorcycles and had gone off on day trips on the weekends.

It was on one such occasion that Carson was relieving himself against a tree when John came over and knelt, taking the rest of Carson's piss in his mouth. He then fondled Carson's dick into hardness. Carson's cock responded by pumping a load of jism down John's throat. Carson then unzipped John's pants and went down on John's cock. It didn't take long for John's cock to reciprocate. The two had been lovers, then partners, ever since. Leather was a natural progression. Carson finally admitted that he liked rough sex and the two began experimenting with whips and paddles, buttplugs and gloved fists. Carson and John realized that it would be exciting to have a group of like-minded men surrounding them and thus, the idea for the Gods of Leather Discipline Club was born.

Their heated session continued with both cocks fully aroused. Both began pumping his cock into the inner recesses of his partner's mouth.

Carson began moaning as he neared climax. He held John's balls in his gloved hands, squeezing on them. John fingered Carson's hole with his gloved hands all the while sucking on the manrod inserted in his mouth.

Leather was rubbing against Leather as the two men continued sucking. The cigars and drinks were forgotten on the tray.

Both men continued a frenzied pumping until both shot a load of cum down each other's throats. It seemed to flow forever.

"Fuck!" moaned Carson as his head reared back, "That felt so damned good."

John continued to lick Carson's dick until every drop was consumed.

The two remained on the floor for some time, kissing, rubbing, pulling heads toward one another's. Gripping their jaws until their tongues were virtually inseparable.

Finally, Carson suggested, "Time to work over our boys? What do you say?"

John stood up and thrust his dick back in his pants, "Well, someone has to do it. Might as well be us."

The two men chuckled as they collected their bags of toys and headed to the dungeon.

The two boys were 'waiting', having been placed in bondage before the Club meeting. The boys were hooded and gagged. Booted and gloved, otherwise deliciously naked. Their heads turned expectantly toward the stairs, even though they couldn't see the Leathermen.

Carson and John laced each other's executioners' hoods into place. They took off their motorcycle jackets and hung them on hooks nearby. Their harnesses outlined their muscled chests.

John chose to work over the boy in the Leather sling. Carson wanted some flogging time with the boy who was manacled to the St. Andrew's Cross. The boy was facing the wall.

And the sessions began.

John began a flogging of the boy's upper torso, making sure that he caught the boy's nipples with the Leather tails. Carson enjoyed seeing a boy's ass redden with his flogger and so he concentrated his efforts on the boy's cute ass.

For some time, there was nothing but the sounds of the repeated strikes of the Leather floggers as they found their targets and made their marks on the willing boys.

Both Leathermen were getting hard-ons as they continued their work.

The boys were good subjects- not flinching or moaning, yet.

Carson pulled a mean fucker off the shelf of toys. It had metal tips at the end of each tail. He concentrated on the boy's tender asscheeks. The boy began moaning and twisting as each tail connected with his assflesh. John's boy was beginning to feel the accumulated effects of the Leather tails on his torso, but despite that the boy's cock was pulsing, fully erect.

John pulled the boy further down into the sling so that his ass was arched upward. He then pulled off the studded belt from his pants and doubling it up, began striking the asscheeks of the young man. The young man reacted, yelping as best he could with a gag in his mouth.

When the boys' asses were sufficiently reddened, both Leathermen retrieved a pair of rubber gloves. Greasing them with lubricant, their fists explored the young men's holes. Both boys flinched and moaned as the fists found their way up each of the boy's fuckholes. Both Leathermen stretched the boy's holes with their fists. When each felt that the hole was ready for the receipt of a manrod, Carson's cock and John's cock eased up the boy's holes.

Both Leathermen's cocks were fully aroused as the cocks made their way up each boy's hole. Both men began moaning as their cocks advanced, finding further and further passageway.

Their pumping began. A slow and steady pump. Prolong it, prolong the fucking. Carson reached around and began pulling on his boy's dick. The boy's dick hardened with the touch of Carson's gloved hand. The lubricant slid up and down the boy's shaft. With the other lubed hand, Carson grabbed the boy's balls.

Meanwhile, John was manipulating the boy's cock and balls in the sling as he continued to pump his cock in the boy's hole. The boy's head was rolling from side to side and he was first to shoot a spray of jism. Witnessing the boy's ejaculation made John pump even harder until he climaxed within the boy's hole.

Carson was pumping harder and harder, slamming his body against the boy and the two soon climaxed. The boy's cum sprayed against the dungeon wall as Carson's cum shot up the boy's ass.

The two Leathermen left their cocks intact for some time, until their cocks were restored to normal size. They withdrew their cocks. The boys were both breathing heavily.

"What a good fuck!" John exclaimed.

The two Leathermen kissed and then unmanacled the two willing boys.

They led the boys upstairs where they were given water. They were then instructed to assume sub positions on all fours. The two Leathermen propped their feet on the boys' backs and smoked the remainder of their cigars. After the Leathermen had finished their smokes and consumed fresh drinks, the boys were re-manacled and led to cots where they would spend the night. Their arms and legs were attached to heavy rings imbedded in the walls of the sleeping room.

The two Leathermen retired to the Master bedroom and fell asleep in each other's arms. Tomorrow was another delicious day of fucking boys.

ALLEY GATHERING

The men of the Gods of Leather Discipline met the following Saturday at the Club Headquarters. They marched in, their heavy boots clumping on the wooden floor. The submissive boys were not in attendance for this was a private meeting.

Carson and John had gotten very little sleep the previous few nights, working on the two boys who were still their captive submissives.

All twelve members were present. It was a day of harvesting.

"All right, Leathermen. Today is the first harvest day for a crop of submissives. We'll split up into groups of three. Go to your favorite haunts. Seek out suitable candidates. We'll rendezvous at 1800 hours," Carson announced. "Grab what gear you need and head out, men."

The Leathermen headed to the supply closet, taking a liberal supply of duct tape, bondage rope, hoods, and other assorted paraphenalia needed for the capture of young men, willing or unwilling.

Rick, Chuck and Jim, as three of the charter members, had participated in several of the runs and always enjoyed working together. They cruised a certain alley which was rich with handsome young men, hustlers, who were always looking for tricks. The three rode off on their cycles with hardened cocks in their pants. The day promised to be a day of excitement as they roared through the streets.

It took them a good half hour to reach their destination. But the day was mild and it was a great day to be riding a cycle. It should be a good day for plucking young cherry asses too.

Lots of people were out on the street so the capture would have to be done discreetly. The fucking cops were out on foot patrol, most of them with big bellies (too many doughnuts) and attitudes to match.

The G.O.L.D men dismounted from their cycles and cruised slowly toward the alley. They drew attention no matter where they went, dressed in full Leather- announcing that they were not men to be fucked with. As they turned left into the alley, several business men in suits quickly scattered. Boys appeared in several doorways. Most of them in tight tee shirts and worn jeans. The jeans were worn in all the right places, offering cock and ass. One boy was down on his knees giving a blowjob- he stopped only momentarily to view the Leathermen before resuming his duties. The businessman looked nervously at the Leathermen striding toward him. He attempted to pull his cock out of the boy's mouth but the boy was unwillingly to give up his fee. The man tossed some bills at the boy and zipping his cock back into his pants, fled the alley. The three men surrounded the boy.

"Blow jobs. $50," the boy stated.

"Stand up, boy," Chuck commanded.

"I do it better on my knees," the boy explained.

"I don't say it twice, boy...," Chuck stated and with that, reached under the boy's arms and pulled him up.

The three men eyed the boy. "Nice build," Jim remarked. Rick turned him around. "Decent ass," he offered as he squeezed the asscheeks through the thin layer of denim with his gloved hands. Chuck squeezed the boy's dick and balls and concluded "Acceptable equipment." The boy was boyishly handsome with blonde hair falling over his watery-blue eyes.

The three men plied the boy with questions. "You ever taken it up the ass, boy?" "How many men do you suck off in a night, boy?" "You belong to anyone, boy?"

The boy was becoming increasingly nervous with all the questions as the muscled Leathermen drew a tighter circle around him.

"Listen, what do you want? You want me to service your Club members- is that it? I could do that- it's still $50 per guy," the boy offered.

The Leathermen just laughed at him, as each of them began manipulating their cods. Their rods were already hardened.

"Let's try you out, boy, see if you are worth fifty bucks," Rick said as he unsnapped his cod. He pushed the boy to his knees and jammed his cock in the boy's mouth. The boy began slurping on the manrod.

"Slow it down, boy. Give me your best tongue worship."

The two other men were rubbing their gloved hands against their extended codpieces.

The boy did develop a slower rhythm as he swallowed the head and the shaft of Rick's cock.

"Good boy," Rick said encouragingly as he pushed the boy's head into his crotch.

Horny as hell, the two other Leathermen unsnapped their cods and began stroking their meat. Rick's cock glided in and out of the boy's mouth with an increased frenzy. He jacked off and before the boy had a chance to lick off all the jism, Chuck guided his cock into the boy's mouth and quickly ejaculated. Jim repeated the process.

The boy continued to kneel in front of the men as they wiped off their cum-covered cocks and placed them back in their respective pouches.

The boy quietly said, "That will be a hundred and fifty…"

The Leathermen just laughed. "Come and get it, boy. Which one of us do you want to take it from?" Rick taunted.

"Come on… I serviced you. What more do you want?" the boy questioned.

"We'll explain that to you later, boy," Chuck remarked as he pulled a pair of handcuffs off his back belt and manacled the boy's hands behind him.

"What the fuck? Let me out of these… you fucking asshole," the boy said in a panicked voice. He started struggling.

Jim, the practical one of the three, had carried a small bag of supplies with him. He tore off a piece of duct tape and placed it squarely over the boy's mouth. The boy's eyes registered more panic as he struggled more vigorously.

"Calm down, asshole," Rick asserted, as he slapped the boy across the face. The boy calmed, for the moment.

"Score one for the team," Jim concluded as the Leathermen slapped each other's backs, "Let's see what else the alley has to offer."

Chuck and Jim flanked the first captive of the day as Rick led the way further down the alley. The boy struggled but received a sharp punch in the stomach each time he did so.

Further down the alley, several boys were watching the procession. Most avoided eye contact. One, however, stood defiantly with his legs spread apart. He was handsome, dark hair with a rim beard and a mustache. He wore a Leather jacket over his tee shirt. A noticeable bulge was evident in his tight jeans.

"You guys look like you want to have some fun," he remarked as they circled around him.

"Yeah, we're looking for fun. We have one pig, but we need two." Jim remarked.

"How much you guys offering?" the boy asked.

"No money, but a time you'll never forget," Chuck replied.

"Fuck, I don't do it for no money, man," the boy responded.

"What if we say you do?" Rick replied, as the men formed a tighter circle around him.

"Ahh, I made a mistake... you guys have a nice day," as he attempted to break past the circle. He was grabbed by Rick and thrown against the brick wall.

"No, listen, I thought you guys were..." the boy started.

"Shut the fuck up. Get down on your knees," Chuck ordered.

The boy complied as he looked up with uncertainty.

The three Leathermen posed the same questions to the handsome young man. He answered them with politeness, addressing them as "Sir" after each question.

"We're looking for suitable candidates for a Club we belong to," Rick began.

"A Motorcycle Club? Huh? I ride..." the boy offered, attempting to get in their good graces.

"Well, something like that, but the men in our Club like to ride young men for pleasure," Rick replied, as his eyes twinkled with sadistic pleasure.

"Oh, oh, well... that's probably not for me..." the boy responded.

"We'll tell you if you are suitable for us or not, now pull down your pants," Jim said, as he unbuttoned the boy's jeans.

"No, really, gotta go... nice talking to you, but I really..." the boy said in a pleading manner.

By this time, his pants had fallen down around his ankles. His cock had shrunken, apparently from fright.

"Look at that, men, the boy's cock has shriveled up. It looks like it needs some watering," Chuck remarked as he unsnapped his cod. He proceeded to piss on the boy aiming at his face, but dousing his chest and crotch. The Leathermen laughed at the sight of the drenched boy.

"Fuck," Rick said, "it reminds me that I gotta take a piss too." All three men took pisses. The other captive watched all this and struggled each time he was handed off to two of the guys for safekeeping. They were stronger than he was and never loosened their grip on the boy.

The second boy was drenched. He had been subdued. He knelt silently as the pair of handcuffs from Jim's toy bag was quickly clicked into place.

With two captives, the Leathermen headed back to their cycles. With their hands manacled behind them, they were loaded on two of the cycles, duct tape securing their arms and feet to the framework of the cycles.

With that, the three cycles left the harvesting location. Chuck, riding solo, rode last in case the boys tried anything stupid. The cycles thundered back to the G.O.L.D. Club.

COP CAPTURE

While Rick, Chuck, and Jim were busy capturing their prey, another trio was headed to the east end of town. They weren't sure where to look- two of them had never been on a harvest run, but were excited to do so. Snake was the third. Called Snake because of the snake tattoo which meandered across his shoulder, its tail on his shoulder blade, its fanged mouth poised to bite off his left nipple. Snake was a charter member and enjoyed the thrill of the hunt. He was a wild card- wild in his sexual tastes, unpredictable, some would say crazy. Once you got to know Snake, however, he was your friend for life. Loyal. Perfect for a brotherhood of Leathermen. And a fucking good mechanic too. Could size up a motorcycle's problems from miles away.

The Leathermen cruised down the highway- the highway was not terribly busy for the time of day. Snake opened his cycle up and soon was going twenty-five miles over the speed limit. The other Leathermen had no choice but to accelerate to the same speed. They didn't know where Snake was going and had never 'harvested' before. He took the Boulevard exit which placed him on a two lane highway- he just assumed the other two guys- Butch and Mark- were following him. He actually did slow down as he approached the outskirts of the small town. Didn't want to draw too much attention to himself, just in case there was a cute young boy to be taken- by surprise.

Butch and Mark caught up to him and they cruised through town at a respectable limit.

"Slim pickings," thought Butch, as he looked at the people out doing their morning errands. They all seemed to be headed to the post office or exiting from it.

"Nothing here," thought Snake as he gunned his engine and departed the one horse town. Open highway and Snake couldn't resist. He opened his Harley up and sped down the open road. Butch and Mark had no choice but to follow as fast as they could. Three or four miles out of town, Snake crested a hill at top speed only to view a cop car sitting on the side of the road. "Oh, Shit," he thought, as he attempted to throttle it down. Butch and Mark would be cresting the hill at top speed, he thought quickly and so, he roared past the cop car at breakneck speed. Butch thought, "That crazy fool- he's making a run for it. Well, guess I'd better go for it too." Not one to be left behind, Mark followed suit.

Snake kept looking in his rearview mirror for a cop's flashing lights and siren, but nothing. Butch and Mark kept careful watch, but still nothing.

"What the hell? I'd like to mix it up with a cop this morning. Give the fucker some lip." He eased his Harley off to the side of the road. Butch and Mark did the same.

Snake dismounted his bike and raised his hands in a questioning manner.

"Don't know, bro, he was in his car, just sitting there," Mark commented.

"Maybe he's playing with himself," offered Butch.

"Did he look like someone we'd want to play with?" Snake asked.

"Hell, we were going at like seventy-five miles per hour, you fucker, and we're supposed to tell you the size of his dick," Mark replied.

Still no cop car had appeared.

"I say, we go back and investigate," Snake said. Snake had a big heart and was willing to help anyone, even if it was a cop.

The other two Leathermen were reluctant, but Snake was the leader and they had to follow his lead.

They mounted their bikes and turned around. As they approached, the cop car was still sitting there. They pulled off to the side of the road. As he saw them approach, the cop drew his gun. "Stay right there. Don't come any closer." After all, three bikers, in heavy Leather, would look intimidating to almost everyone.

"Hey, Buddy. We're just trying to help," Snake answered, "You have car trouble? I'm a mechanic."

The cop was not convinced. After all, a big bullish man in full Leather was walking toward him. He continued to point the gun at Snake.

"What happened?" Snake continued.

"It just stopped- alternator light is on. Won't turn over."

"Well, it could be almost anything- dead battery, alternator, out of gas. Let me take a look. Pop the hood."

The cop obliged. Within minutes, Snake had diagnosed the problem. "You ain't goin' nowhere, man. Your car is as dead as road kill."

The cop began to relax a bit. He eased the gun down and apparently put it back in his holster.

"Come here, I'll show you." The cop reluctantly got out of the patrol car and joined Snake under the hood. Transmission fluid had leaked out of the transmission- a large green puddle was visible under the car. The battery connections were corroded. The fan belt looked like a well-worn rubber band.

"Man, why did you let your car get in this condition?"

"I was just hired last week. This is the car they assigned me. Hell, they didn't even give me a working radio. I've been trying to reach headquarters."

For the first time, Snake looked at the young cop. A young stud- military crew cut, tight tan uniform, with a very handsome chest squeezed into his uniform shirt. Nice tight butt. Military boots with the pant legs tucked into the top of them. Fresh out of training, Snake assumed.

"So, what's your plan of action, Buddy?" Snake questioned.

"I just have to sit and wait for someone to come and get me. I can't abandon Police Department property."

"Well, hell, you're screwed. Where's your Department?"

"Thirty miles in the direction you were headed."

"We could give you a lift, Buddy."

"I told you I can't abandon the car."

Snake was getting a little riled at the cop. He was offering help and the boy refused it.

"We could take you back into town and you could call your department."

"I can't abandon the car…"

Snake was about ready to say "Well, then fuck you," when he took a second look at the handsome young man in front of him.

"What would happen if you did abandon the car?"

"They would strip me of my uniform."

"Hmmm," was Snake's simple reply as he motioned Butch and Mark over to the cop car.

The three Leathermen surrounded the youthful cop. He looked from one set of eyes to another. He began sweating as the men closed in on him. One grabbed his arms and quickly had them secured behind his back. Butch pulled a piece of duct tape from his bag of supplies and covered the cop's mouth. The boy began struggling but he was no match for three burly Leathermen.

"With that last comment, you certainly gave me an idea, son."

Snake began rubbing his gloved hand across the boy's chest. With the other hand, he squeezed the boy's basket. It was nice and tight.

Butch pressed his loaded cod against the cop's tight ass.

"Not here, not now. A car could come by at any minute. Let's get him secured on the back of my cycle," Snake ordered.

They secured him on the back of Snake's cycle. Fortunately, Snake knew the back roads in the area and they zipped along without notice. As a precaution, Snake placed his helmet over the boy's face so that anyone passing by would not notice the taped mouth of the cop they were transporting.

Snake led the way but not to Club Headquarters The Leathermen had captured a prize and before they turned the boy over to the Club, he wanted to have some fun. Snake knew instinctively that Mark and Butch would play along. Snake led the way to his own dungeon, appropriately named the 'Snake Pit'.

The men parked in Snake's yard and unloaded their captured prey. Snake led the way down the steps to the basement dungeon, fully outfitted with a workover table, a sling, a St. Andrew's Cross, and a wall of floggers, dildos and assorted toys.

The boy was really panicked by this time and wrestled with Butch and Mark as he was led into the dark interior of the dungeon.

"Strap him down on the table. Face-down. Hood him."

With some more spirited wrestling, the boy was strapped into place with heavy Leather bondage straps. No one had ever escaped them.

The Leathermen couldn't keep their hands off of the cop. They slapped his asscheeks through the twilled fabric of the uniform pants. They laid a single tail across his back and despite the uniform shirt and tee shirt, it still stung like hell. The boy's protests were muffled by the black Leather hood which was tightly laced around his head. A buttplug gag was inserted in his mouth. The eyeholes were zippered shut.

Snake reached underneath the boy to loosen his trousers. He pulled them down around the boy's knees along with his underpants. He groped, finding a large cock and low-hanging balls. Despite his fear, the boy had a larger-than-normal cock. Snake placed that in his memory bank for future use.

He pulled a cat-o-nine tails flogger off the wall. He began a rigorous flogging of the boy's virgin ass. The boy moaned and wrestled against the Leather straps.

His ass was soon reddened with the strap marks of the flogger.

Snake relinquished the flogger to Mark, who continued the ass beating.

Snake stood to the side, lighting a big cigar.

When Mark handed Butch the flogger, Butch returned it to the wall and instead chose a wooden paddle.

The paddle made a satisfying cracking sound with each strike and the boy flinched, rearing upward with each strike.

The session continued until the boy's ass was a field of red marks, expertly laid by the three sadistic Leathermen.

Snake pulled an inflatable dildo off the wall and lubricated it with some lube. He shoved it up the unsuspecting hole of the boy. The boy moaned, crying out in a muffled cry.

Snake grinned to his two fellow Leathermen. "Boy's a virgin, I think."

Once the dildo was inserted, Snake pumped it up, inflating the artificial cock further up the boy's passage.

Butch and Mark stood silently observing, waiting for their turn. They puffed on cigars.

One by one, the dildo was replaced by the three men's own inflatable cocks, which hardened as soon as they achieved entry. All three Leathermen were horny as fuck and wanted to prolong their time in the boy's hole. All three came quickly-the excitement accelerating them toward climax sooner than they had hoped The boy was a perfect candidate for sadists. He squirmed and flinched, moaned and groaned, making the Leathermen hornier than they already were. A complacent boy could be pretty dull.

HOG TIME

'Mad' Max led the third team of harvesters. If Snake was considered a wild one, Max was an even wilder loose cannon. He was a Leatherman and damned fucking proud of it. Don't get in his way, mutha fucker, or he would happily throw you on the floor and plow your ass with his big cock. Max was a big man. Proud of his tattoos, proud of his piercings. If you were interested, even if you weren't interested, he would be glad to show off the fucking big ring piercing his cock's head. He might then pin you to a wall and stick his cock where the sun 'don't shine'. Max was a veteran, a survivor of the Vietnam War. It had exacted its toll, he had lost his right leg up to the kneecap. Hell, he'd show you his artificial leg too. Max had his strong fetishes. Leather wasn't one of them. Leather was his lifestyle and he wore it every damned day he was alive. Well-worn pants and old comfortable boots. Usually his harness, muscle bands, a vest, his mirrored sunglasses, cycle gauntlets, and his Muir cap were worn too. Max had a shortly-cropped brown mustache and beard and a mass of brown curly hair on his head. Weighing over two hundred seventy five pounds, Max was an imposing figure. He wasn't afraid of anybody, but many were afraid of him.

As said, Max did have his fetishes. He loved to ram his meaty fist or his swollen, large cock up a boy's ass. He just laughed when they started squealing or begging for him to stop. He took what he wanted from a boy. And there were only a few things a boy was good for. An appropriate receptacle for a Leatherman's cock was first and foremost.

Max was a natural-born cycle rider. Max was only two years old when he was strapped to his Father's motorcycle and taken for his first motorcycle ride. His Father often told him of that ride and how Max had squealed with delight. He had learned a lot from his old man [God Rest His Soul]- killed in a cycle accident when Max was thirteen. Despite the arguments put forth by the family members, it was his Father's express wish that Max inherit his Father's Harley, made in the year 1957. Max cherished that cycle, had it in excellent repair and took it out occasionally. When he returned from Vietnam, Max had received disability payments as regular as clockwork- he bought his own Harley from those payments. "Hell, the government owed me something- after all, I gave 'em a leg." Max had customized his cycle- he looked like the fuckin' 'Easy Rider' speeding down the road. And despite the Club rules, he liked to travel alone. But, for the mission, he was on good behavior. After all, he was riding with two handsome fuckers- Mick and de Lorenzo. de Lorenzo was known by his last name. He had some God-awful first name like Homer or Elmer. "Or some sorry-ass name. No wonder he wants to go by his last name," Max thought. And de Lorenzo would become belligerent if you did call him by his first name. He'd probably fist you if you did. Of course, if that's what you wanted, it was a great way to get fisted.

Max led the three away from the Club, but their journey was the shortest of all. They were to be the Review Committee to interview the guy in the Leather store and the other candidate.

Just a few minutes later, they dismounted and headed into the store. The smell of Leather was overpowering and the guys' cocks responded by hardening in their Leather pants.

The boy was busy putting out a new shipment of lube and looked up only momentarily to say, "Hi, Guys. Let me know if I can be of help."

The guys eyed him from where he stood. He was slender but as Rick had indicated, he wore Leather. He wore a pair of asstight pants, which when he turned around were laced at the crotch. "Not much of a bulge," de Lorenzo thought, "You think it would be 'rising' to the occasion when he saw us." Rationalizing the situation, however, he realized that this guy probably viewed Leatherguys every day in the store.

Max sauntered over to him. He was an imposing figure.

"Yes, Sir?"

"We're from the Review Committee of G.O.L.D. Did Rick say anything to you?" The boy stopped arranging the bottles of lube.

"What do you mean?"

"Oh, never mind, boy. Just a thought. How about showing us the stock room?" By this time, Max stood with his booted feet flanking the boy's booted feet.

"Well, Sir, I can't. I'm the only one on duty. The manager had to mail out some orders."

"Well, good, son, then he won't mind if you take a little break."

"But the store, Sir...." the boy began as de Lorenzo went over to the front door and threw the dead bolt.

"Hey, you can't do that," the boy protested.

By this time, Mick had pinioned the boy's arms behind his back and Max's cock bulge was thrusting itself into the boy's crotch area.

"Who says we can't?"

The three men escorted the boy to the back room where he was forced onto his knees.

Max massaged his codpiece and then ripped it off. His large cock sprang forward, slapping the boy on the cheek.

"Suck me off, boy."

The boy looked defiantly up at Max but opened his mouth. The cock, seeking a warm, juicy tonguefuck, hardened inside the boy's mouth. Max pulled the boy's head toward the base of his cock. Once the boy had accepted the fact that he was going to suck Max off, he did a damned decent job. The boy had some experience as a cocksucker as Rick had indicated at the initial meeting. Max was not shy about letting his sexual feelings known. He began pumping his cock in the boy's mouth, yelling "Atta boy. Take that meat! Take my manrod, you cocksucking bitch! All the way, boy. Don't you let up, boy. You take my fucking cock and you get me off. Fuck, boy, that feels good. Get me good and wet. You know where it's going after you get it all greased up." The man's massive hands were clamping the sides of the boy's head. He pushed the boy's head further and further until the whole cock was in the boy's mouth, Max's big balls slapping against the boy's chin. The boy was breathing through his nose, there was so much cockmeat in his mouth. "Fuck, yeah, boy. Suck me off. Do it."

Mick and de Lorenzo stood patiently, waiting for their turn. But Max knew how to prolong his climax. Edge-play. Just when he was about ready to shoot, he'd pull his cock out. Slap the boy roughly on his cheek. "I want it to be harder than this, you fuck-up!" His cock was already immense. He'd jam it back in and the boy would vacuum the cock harder.

Mick and de Lorenzo's cocks were already pulled out of their Leather pants and they were stroking each other's meat.

"Fuck, yeah, boy, get this Leatherman's dick harder," Max said, as he pushed the cock in the boy's mouth repeatedly.

Max had an iron grip on the back of the boy's head and wouldn't relent on the grip. The boy had no choice but to tongue and suck as best he could.

Mick and de Lorenzo were doing a frenzied pumping.

Max began moaning. His head reared back, his back arched and with one final thrust, he shot an immense load of cum down the boy's throat.

"FUCK!" Max yelled. The boy was gasping for air as he tried to swallow as much of it as he could. Some spilled out on his lips and dribbled down his chin. Max was breathing heavily from the exertion, but he didn't release the boy's head. He pumped his cock in and out of the boy's mouth until the boy had licked most of the dew off of his shaft.

"Fuck, yeah. Hell, that felt good, boy." He patted the boy roughly on the back of his head.

"He'll do," Max said.

"Hey, we're not sure… we haven't had a chance to test him out." Mick picked up the slight boy and laid him on a nearby table. His legs dangled off the end of the table, his ass arched upward. Mick roughly pulled the boy's pants down around his knees after he had unlaced the crotch of the boy's pants. The boy's cock was thin and long, and erect.

Mick spit on his gloved hand, fingered the boy's hole, and jammed his excited cock up the boy's hole. de Lorenzo headed to the front of the table. He pried the boy's mouth open and was soon pumping his cock into the same hole that had just taken Max's jism.

Max looked on, taunting the boy, "You sure as hell are good at customer service, boy."

Mick was pumping his cock up the boy's hole. The boy's ass expanded and contracted, accepting Mick's cock further and further. The boy was doing a damned decent job on de Lorenzo's throbbing rod as well.

By this time, Max's cock was recovering, hardening despite the big load he had just shot.

The frenzied action continued, Mick's cock pumping in and out of the boy's ass and de Lorenzo's cock being lubricated by the boy's experienced tongue. Max pulling on his throbbing manrod with his left hand. Max wanted a piece of the action. He stood near Mick, reaching under the edge of the table and started pulling on the boy's cock with his right hand. The boy moaned but continued his sucking, his ass expanding and contracting.

de Lorenzo couldn't control his cum any longer and shot a load in the boy's mouth. The boy's cock, being pulled on by the iron grip of Max's hand, shot a stream of cum. Viewing that, Mick made a final thrust and shot a cockload up the boy's ass. Max, horny as hell, shot a second load.

"Yeah, Max, I think he'll do," concluded de Lorenzo. The men laughed. The boy was exhausted but there was a smile on his face.

"Yes, Candidate #1 gets our vote."

The Leathermen helped the boy off the table. He went with them willingly. They didn't even have to manacle him to Max's cycle.

The storeowner, returning shortly thereafter, was puzzled to find the lights on, the front door locked, and Tim gone.

Max led the Leathermen through a labyrinth of roads until he reached their second rendezvous point- the Wayward Inn. It was noted for its seedy, smoky interior and for the guys it attracted- Leathermen. Bikers. Fucking hunks. Max stopped there once in awhile, just to mix things up. Play a game of pool. Kick back a beer. Relax with men of a similar mind. Smoke a cigar even though the fucking state said 'No Smoking'. Fuck 'em. The candidate worked at the Wayward Inn- he was the resident bootblack, Joe. Joe was a boy of about twenty three or twenty four. From what Max had heard- Joe was hung like a horse. Enjoyed doing a little extra for a man who was having his boots shined.

The cycles roared into the parking lot, stirring up quite a bit of dust. There were already a number of cycles out front. The guys marched in, keeping close watch on their initiate from the Leather store.

When they walked in, it was as if they were looking in a mirror. Men in heavy Leather jackets, chaps, boots, fingerless gloves. Lots of chains and spikes. A cloud of smoke hovered near the ceiling. The crack of pool cues against billiard balls were evidence that a spirited game was in session. The guys got their beers and headed for the back section where the bootblack's station was set up. Only he wasn't there.

Max sauntered back out to the bar and when he finally got the bartender's attention, he asked, "Where's Joe?"

"He'll be finished with a client... soon," the bartender replied.

"Yeah, but he's not...," Max started, but winked at the bartender, gave him the thumbs up, and returned to the other three.

"Joe will be back in a few... he's giving somebody some head."

The men stood around sucking on their beers. The three men pulled out cigars and began stoking them. The Leatherboy stood nearby, feeling somewhat awkward until Mick pulled the boy toward him, embracing his shoulder. "Stick with me, boy, you'll be okay."

The men obtained a second round. As they were emptying their second bottles, Joe came out of the basement door. He was followed closely by a Leatherman who simply thanked Joe, pressed a bill in his hand, and left.

"Well, Buddy, business is good I see," Max remarked, somewhat sarcastically.

"Yes, Sir, I can't complain. Business is exceptional," Joe replied. "Another satisfied customer," as he gestured toward the retreating Leatherman.

"You think you can shine these fuckers," Max continued, pointing to his engineer boots. They were pretty dirty with mud caked on them.

"Yes, Sir," Joe said.

"Wouldn't mind you polishing my knob too."

"I'd be more than happy to do that, Sir."

"How about my friends here- you think you can do them too?"

"Gladly, Sir." Joe found de Lorenzo particularly handsome.

Joe seated Max in the elevated chair to have his boots shined. He rubbed them lovingly with his bare hands, spreading the black polish on with the palms of his hands. Max's were the biggest challenge, of course, with all the mud caked on them. He rubbed the black polish on one coat at a time. To Max, it felt like a gentle caressing as Joe massaged the calves, the heel, the toes of his boots.

Max was horny all the time and so, it was no surprise to him that he had an immediate reaction- a hard cock as soon as the bootblack began rubbing the polish into his boots. Max relaxed in the chair as the boy continued. He could feel his cock hardening, knocking at its codpiece for release. He massaged it through his cod. Joe occasionally looked up from his bootblack duties. He could see the thick meat outlined in its Leather pouch. While he continued to rub with one hand, he reached around to his back pocket and pulled out a glove. He put the glove on his right hand. Unsnapping the right side of the cod, Joe began massaging Max's cock with the black Leather gloved hand. The boy played with the Prince Albert piercing, fingering it with his gloved fingers. Masaging the cockhead.

Max's cock was throbbing. "Oh, fuckin' yeah, boy. Stroke that meat of mine. Fuck, that feels good. All the way up the shaft, encircling the head with your Leathered fingers, fucker. And don't forget my boots, boy. Rub the left boot with your hand and rub the right boot with your chest, boy. Atta, boy. Keep stroking my cock, boy. I didn't tell you to stop."

Max was enjoying his session with the bootblack. He'd like to have this sub for his own use. He already had the services of a good boy but what Daddy couldn't use two? Coming home after a day of working at a construction site, sit down in his easy chair, and have this boy massage his cock. He imagined what the boy looked like naked. Big hard meat hanging down between his legs. His naked chest flexing while his hands were massaging Max's booted feet. Max viewed Joe's mouth. Generous mouth. Sucking on my rod, tonguing my balls. Sucking on my pierced nips. Fuck, yeah. This boy has my vote.

With the boy's assistance, Max couldn't hold his jism any longer and shot a load in his cod. The boy dutifully used one of his clean rags to wipe it out. He then brought the cum to his mouth and cleaned the rag. Max breathed a deep sigh of satisfaction.

While Max was being 'pleasured' Mick had taken Tim, the boy from the Leather store, to the alley behind the bar. The boy was instructed to kneel in front of the Leatherman. "Hands behind your back, boy," Mick instructed as he pulled his cock out of his pants. The boy needed no further instruction and was quick to lubricate the man's cock with his tongue. As the boy began stroking Mick's cock with his tongue, Mick gripped the boy's head firmly, bobbing it up and down on the throbbing rod. Mick liked his sex hard and rough. As the boy was sucking him, he thought about the days ahead when he would place this boy in bondage. Truss him up with rope and Leather straps. Facing the wall. Fuck the boy's ass with his enlarged tool. Use his collection of inflatable dildos. Fist him. Have him spread-eagle on a table and work him over. Slap him with paddles. Piss on him. Yeah, he wanted to do that- in an urgent, primeval way. He looked down at the boy. The boy was really going to town- really giving him an excellent cocksucking. The boy had a slender body. But a cute ass- Mick had already felt the pleasure of sticking his manrod up that boy's hole. He wanted more. He wanted to have this boy in his own dungeon for days at a time. The boy might just have to miss a few of the Club meetings for Mick's own pleasures. Mick definitely wanted this boy for his own.

As the boy was edging Mick toward climax, Max appeared in the alley.

"Hell, I wondered what happened to you... I should have known, you horny bastard," said Max, addressing Mick.

Max slapped the boy on the back of his head, driving the boy's head all the way to the base of Mick's shaft. "Chow down, boy. that's tasty cock. At least, that's what I've heard." The boy said nothing. He was too busy eating cock.

de Lorenzo had climbed into the bootblack's chair. Joe looked up at him admiringly. He thought de Lorenzo was so handsome. de Lorenzo was already rubbing his cock through his Leather pants. He propped his right boot up on the footrest. de Lorenzo thought the boy was damned attractive with black tousled hair and innocent blue eyes. Beefy build, with handsome pecs hidden by a black tee shirt. He viewed the boy's cock lodged down the left leg of his black jeans.

"Shine my boot, boy."

"Gladly, Sir. For you, Sir, I will shine them like they have never been shined before."

Joe began rubbing the first coat of polish into the boot's toe, using the palm of his already blackened hand to add the polish.

The rubbing stimulated de Lorenzo's cock, as if the boot polishing was hotwired to his cock. The boy added a coat of polish to the shaft of the boot, rubbing it into place with his chest. The boy removed his tee shirt. His pink nipples exposed among the fur on his chest.

"Fuck, son, you excite me. I want your tongue down my throat," de Lorenzo whispered.

The boy straddled the man and their tongues were soon involved in each other's mouth. The Leatherman pulled the boy closer to him, rubbing the boy's back with his gloved hands. Both were moaning as the sexual tension between the two mounted. de Lorenzo pulled the boy even closer to him, not caring if he got black shoe polish on his Leathers. He would make the boy rub it into his Leathers later. Right now, he wanted the boy's tongue thrust into his mouth as far as he could swallow.

The boy reached down and massaged de Lorenzo's already extended dick. He pulled on the snaps, releasing the cod and de Lorenzo's dick from its Leather enclosure. The boy began stroking the extended manrod. The boy was now reclining in de Lorenzo's lap and de Lorenzo could feel the boy's tool pressing against his. He reached down and unzipped the boy's black jeans. His cock was a good ten inches- hard, firm, mushroom-headed. He began stroking the boy's cock with his gloved hand.

Tongues exploring each other's mouth. Cock against cock. Boy's body pressed against the Leatherman's body. de Lorenzo holding the boy firmly in place with his free hand, the other stroking the boy's cock faster and faster. The boy's hand expertly manipulating the Leatherman's cock.

The sexual heat rising. Tongues exploring every crevice of each other's mouth. The boy being drawn closer and closer to the Leatherman's excited body. Cock meat pressed against throbbing cock meat. de Lorenzo could feel his cum climbing up the shaft of his penis. Joe could feel his cum headed the same route. Their kissing became frenzied, biting each other. Jaws locked. Eyes closed. The thrust of manhood to arrive shortly. Body pressed against body.

And within a few more seconds, a cumload of sperm shot from both cocks, bathing both cocks in man and boy jism. And still the passion continued. Kissing, fondling, groping, squeezing, bodies slammed against one another's.

Finally, the mouths separated. "Fuck, Sir, that was fantastic!" the boy whispered into his lover's mouth. de Lorenzo's eyes twinkled, "Fuck, boy, we're in agreement!". They continued for some time. de Lorenzo knew he wanted this boy as his own personal fuckslave.

RENDEZVOUS WITH A HITCHHIKER

Carson and John had stayed behind to prepare the Club for the eventual receipt of boys- willing and unwilling. The supply closet was slightly bare- because the harvesters had taken handcuffs, wrist restraints, hoods, bondage rope, duct tape, and the like. The two Leathermen had brought some of their own equipment from home- the equipment that wasn't currently in use on their own bondage boys. As the third of their trio they had partnered themselves with Phillippe, a hunky French Canadian bear. He was hairy, muscular and as horny as any of the other men. He could seduce any boy with his accent.

"Gentlemen, are we ready to ride?" Phillippe asked anxiously. He had participated in the last two hunts and had always succeeded in bringing in at least one delicious boy.

"Almost, Buddy," John replied. They continued to survey the Club for readiness. Rubber sheeting had been spread in the darker recesses of the Club for the eventual watersports party that was an initiation for the boys. The refrigerator was stocked with lots of cold beer.

"I think we're ready to ride," Carson concluded as he surveyed the room one last time.

The Leathermen locked the front door and mounted their Harleys- Phillippe rode one too.

Cranking their engines, they peeled out of the parking space. Carson led the way. He had assigned them the west end of town, where there were always a handful of candidates.

As they sped through traffic, the men's cocks hardened. They were ready for some fucking hot action and hoped that they wouldn't be disappointed. They had been riding only about twenty minutes or so when Carson spotted a young man with a huge backpack on his back. He was walking at a slow clip along the shoulder of the road. He wore a motorcycle jacket. Tight ass jeans and cowboy boots. At least they looked pointed from the distance that Carson was viewing him at. They slowed as they came up to the young man. He had turned around and stuck out his thumb. The cyclemen pulled off onto the shoulder and dismounted.

All three men approached the young man. They were not disappointed. A stubble of growth on his handsome jaw, but a shaved head. A loop earring in his right ear. His chest was broad. Phillippe immediately looked at the boy's denimed crotch and noted a muscular dick resting comfortably in the jeans.

"Morning, guys," the hitchhiker called as they approached.

"You need a ride?" Carson asked.

"Sure would like one. Where are you guys headed?"

"Wherever you're headed, Buddy," John replied in a flirtatious tone.

The hitchhiker laughed. He named a town about forty miles away. He explained that he was looking for work and had heard of a job in the town.

"We'll take you there- we have to make a couple of stops along the way," Phillippe explained, his accent thickening.

"Hey, guys, I'd appreciate it. Cowboy boots aren't the easiest boots to be walking in."

"Climb aboard- which one of us do you want to ride with?"

He chose to ride with Phillippe as they climbed back on their cycles and roared down the highway. His backpack was stowed on the back of Carson's cycle.

Mental telepathy, of course, was in play. Carson was the navigator and the spotter for a deserted place to 'interview' the candidate.

About fifteen miles or so down the road, they came to a patch of highway which had some dense vegetation. Carson signaled for them to pull off. An old dirt path led into the thicket of bushes. They parked their bikes there and dismounted.

The hitchhiker didn't question their decision but dismounted at the same time.

"Man, I gotta take a leak," John began.

"Hell, me too. That morning coffee has an effect on you...," Carson said. They began marching into the thicket. The boy followed and Phillippe followed him closely behind.

As the boy began to unzip his pants, Phillippe caught his arms and secured them behind the boy. The boy struggled, "Hey, what the hell?"

"Shut up, boy," Phillippe responded, "We're just out for a little fun."

"Well, don't let me stop you, but let me out of here," the boy continued as he struggled. He was an even match for Phillippe and he broke away from his grip. Carson and John lunged for him and tackled him around his legs. He fell facedown into the brush.

While he was down, the men tied several loops of bondage rope around his ankles. They gagged him with a black bandana. John and Carson lifted him upright and secured him to a sturdy sapling- slender but sturdy.

The boy was struggling, attempting to yell.

"I said settle down, NOW!" Phillippe demanded as he slapped the boy hard across the face more than a few times.

The boy attempted to spit out the black bandana but it was firmly entrenched in the boy's mouth, tied tightly in back. He continued to struggle against his bondage ropes.

Carson unzipped the boy's jacket. A handsome chest strained against the grey tee-shirt which was stained with perspiration.

"Fuck, let him rest for a few minutes. I can hold my piss a little longer." John informed his buddies.

They stood off to one side and watched the boy continue to struggle. Despite the mission, they were all smirking with satisfaction. Another boy captured.

The boy continued to struggle for some time until John announced, "I can't hold my piss any longer."

He marched over to the boy and with some effort (and the help of Carson), got him down on his knees, still tightly confined to the trunk of the tree.

He looked the victim in the face and warned him, "I'm taking out your gag, but you scream once and it goes back in. Understand me, boy?"

The boy nodded.

The gag was removed and as the Leatherman predicted, the captured boy started screaming.

John massaged his big cock and aimed his stream of piss toward the screaming mouth. The boy sputtered as the piss drenched his face, some of it landing in the boy's mouth, causing him to stop screaming.

Carson had pulled out his pissladen cock and took over when John had finished. More piss shot into the boy's mouth and he kept gulping as it found its way down his throat.

Finally, Phillippe pulled out his bullcock. It was heavy with more Leatherman's piss.

By now, the boy's head was drooping. Phillippe had to jerk the boy's jaw upward before inserting his giant cock in the boy's mouth.

"Don't bite my cock or you will have more than you bargained for." With that, he let loose an endless stream.

He seemed to piss forever.

The boy's face and tee shirt were drenched in man's piss.

"Please...," the boy pleaded, "let me go, I won't say anything to anybody. Just let me go." The boy was shaking as he delivered this promise.

"Ah, hell, son, we're just having a little fun with you. Bet after all this piss, you gotta take a leak too."

With some difficulty, the men lifted the boy back up to a standing position.

Carson unzipped the boy's pants and was greeted with a raging hard-on. His cock was a good eight inches. It bobbed up and down. John couldn't resist and swatted it several times. "It's like a damned boomerang..." John said and the three men laughed.

Carson began massaging the boy's cock with his gloved hand. The cock pulsed. You could actually see the veins in his cock throbbing.

Carson stood in front of the young man and clenched the boy's cock between his two legs. He pulled the boy's jaw upward and thrust his tongue in the boy's mouth.

Despite his fear, the boy's tongue began exploring Carson's mouth.

"Damn, this boy has done this a few times," Carson remarked as he reinserted his tongue in the boy's mouth. He began rubbing the boy's shoulders, reaching under his cycle jacket to massage the shoulder blades. The boy's cock continued to pulse. Carson could feel it through his Leathers.

John stood behind Carson and reaching between Carson's legs, began teasing the boy's cockhead with his gloved hands. It seemed to lengthen. Throbbing. Rising.

Carson jammed his tongue in the boy's mouth even further and the boy began moaning.

Phillippe did not want to miss out on the action. He stood on the other side of the tree and grabbed the boy's asscheeks. What he really wanted to do was to jam his bullcock up the boy's asshole, but the damned tree was in the way.

He continued to massage the boy's asscheeks. The boy's cock began a slow rhythmic sliding back and forth between Carson's legs.

The boy closed his eyes. Carson continued his tonguing of the boy's mouth, with the boy's tongue exploring Carson's mouth.

The boy's cock slid back and forth, increasing in intensity. John caught the cockhead each time, exploring the piss slit with his gloved fingers.

The boy began pumping his cock. Phillippe grabbed onto the hitchhiker's asscheeks and echoed the motions of the boy's body. John fingered the piss slit. Carson continued to explore the boy's mouth. His cock was pressing against his Leather cod.

The boy pumped and pumped. He began breathing heavily. With a muffled "Fuck" he shot a load of jism which shot out between Carson's legs.

A portion of it landed on John's gloved hands.

The action continued until the boy stopped pumping. He was breathing in ragged breaths.

"Good boy," Carson announced as he pulled his tongue out of the boy's mouth.

The boy continued to breathe heavily as the Leathermen stepped away and stroked their own hard rods.

They allowed the boy to resume normal breathing before they informed him that that was just foreplay.

The boy didn't respond. He surely knew what was coming next.

He was once again positioned down on his knees, still tightly tied to the tree.

One by one, an overexcited cock was pushed into his mouth. Each had a load of cum to deliver to the boy's throat. Phillippe waited until last.

His big bullcock was pulled out of his Leathercod dripping with precum.

The boy nearly choked on the cock as it was thrust into his mouth. He did the best he could in swallowing the immense dick.

It didn't take long for Phillippe to come. He usually enjoyed prolonging a sucking session, but this was his first cocksucking of the day. He shot an immense load of cum down the boy's throat.

They let the boy recuperate. He was drenched in drying piss. His cock was covered with his own drying cum, and now, cum was dribbling out of the corners of his mouth.

The Leathermen conferred and agreed that the young hitchhiker was a good candidate for their submissive boy training- willing or unwilling, that remained to be seen. Phillippe repositioned the boy so that was now tied tightly to the tree. Black bandana in his mouth.

Carson explained to the boy, "We're going to leave you here..." The boy shook his head violently and his body began trembling.

Carson slapped the boy roughly across the face, "Just for a little while. We have some business to attend to. We'll pick you up on the way back. You're just too much of a risk, boy. Bondage will do you good. It will settle you down." Carson retrieved a black Leather hood from his cycle and laced it tightly over the boy's head. The hitchhiker was left to contemplate his future as a captive Leather boy.

The Leathermen marched back to their cycles and headed on to their next captive, wherever he might be.

BACK AT THE CLUB

Rick, Chuck and Jim were the first to arrive back at the Club. Rick unlocked the door as the other two struggled with the captives.

"Looks like Carson and John have prepared for this afternoon's activities."

They wrestled the two hustlers into the darkest part of the Club. The two boys were quickly manacled to heavy wooden posts, numbered #1 and #2. Chuck retrieved the equipment from the men's cycles and the two boys were quickly hooded with black Leather hoods. The mouths were zippered shut. Before the evening, if the harvest was successful, there would be five more hooded candidates.

"You guys want a beer?" asked Jim as he retrieved a beer from the well-stocked refrigerator.

"Hell, yeah. Gotta have something to suck on," replied Chuck.

Jim offered, "I got something you can suck on, bitch" as he rubbed his cock in his pants.

Chuck sauntered over, poking Jim's crotch with the lip of his beer bottle. He fondled the outline of Jim's cock with his gloved hand. The cock responded by visibly hardening within Jim's Leathers.

Soon, the two were in a locked embrace. Jim's naked cock against the hardened rod still in Chuck's pants.

Chuck led Jim to one of the posts and pressed Jim's back against it.

Chuck was still manipulating Jim's cock, pulling on it. As he pulled on it, he whispered, "Yeah, I want it, bitch. I want you to be my pussy boy."

Jim replied, "You want it? You cocksucking whore. I'll give it to you, but up your fuckable ass."

Rick returned from the supply closet only to find the two in a lover's embrace. He merely shook his head and readied some more equipment that the Leathermen would need.

The two Leathermen continued to play. Jim unzipped Chuck's pants and pulled out his partner's swollen rod.

He squeezed on it. The head was enlarged with a drop of dew in the piss slit.

"Looks like your pussy is dripping, boy," Jim taunted

"Fuck you, it ain't because of you with your two inch rammer," said Chuck.

"You fucking bitch," Jim replied as he squeezed Chuck's cock harder and harder. Despite Chuck's efforts, he couldn't control his cum and he soon shot, aiming it for Jim's cock. Some of it landed on Jim's cock serving as a lubricant and it was only a matter of minutes before Jim's cock erupted.

The Leathermen swabbed the cock cream off of each other's cocks and fed it to one another.

Once satisfied, they resumed their duties of getting the Club ready.

The two trussed-up boys stood quietly. They didn't have much choice. Hooded and manacled. Dried cum and piss on their bodies and clothing. Before the night was through, they would be covered in both. They didn't realize that the initiation lasted four nights.

The boys looked very inviting, just ripe for the picking. Rick sauntered over to the two boys. He squeezed each boy's cock through the boy's denim. The cocks were both fairly hard. Even though he wanted to play with them, he felt that he had to restrain himself. "Shit," he thought as he rubbed his Leathered cock against the front of the first hustler's pants. "I have my needs..." He massaged the boy's ass. The boy's head was rolling from side to side.

"Damn, I want some cock in my hand," as he pulled the boy's swollen cock out of his pants.

The cock was hardened. Rick roughly slapped it with his gloved hand. It responded by getting longer and arching upward.

He twisted the boy's cock, his gloved fingers wrapping around the boy's balls.

He began pulling on them. They were hanging loose and pliable.

He began stroking the cock with his left hand, pulling on it in an upward stroke.

The boy was moaning through the black Leather hood. His eyes were closed behind the hood.

Rick pulled out his own cock and held the two cocks tightly together. Stroking both of them now with an upward jerk. The boy's arms flexed as his chest contracted.

Rick continued to stroke, harder and harder, pulling on the two cocks.

He was breathing heavily as he knew he was going to shoot soon. He increased the stroking and two geysers shot forth, lubricating the dicks with cum.

He continued stroking them in their creamy lube.

"Oh, fuck, I needed that," as he unzipped the mouth of the hood and inserted his cum-covered glove into the boy's mouth.

The boy licked on the glove and seemed pleased to receive the other glove as soon as the first was cleaned.

Rick left the boy's pants around his ankles. He wouldn't need clothing on for quite a while.

Rick was pleasured for the moment, but he looked over at the other boy. The other boy stood silently by. He wanted him too but he thought "Duty prevails... for the moment.".

He returned to the Club's main section. Jim and Chuck both had knowing smirks on their faces.

"Just couldn't resist a little boy, could you now? You horny bastard," remarked Chuck.

"Just testing the candidate for suitability," Rick replied.

"Yeah, right," Jim replied, as the three guys relaxed with cigars and beer.

"Why don't we cruise for a while?" suggested Chuck.

They finished their beers and mounted their cycles. It was a flawless day and too good a day to waste in the confines of the Club. They left the boys to settle in. They headed out, looking for some activity to mix it up for awhile.

About half an hour after the three Leathermen had departed, Snake, Butch and Mark arrived at the Club. Their captor was not going easily.

He struggled as he was placed on Butch's cycle after the session at Snake's 'Pit'. The two remaining men rode in back of Butch's cycle which was carrying the captured. The boy squirmed and wrestled even while the cycle was in motion at fifty-five miles per hour.

"Damned fool," Snake thought, "he's gonna fall off the damned cycle."

Fortunately, it was only a ten or fifteen minute ride to the Club. Snake unlocked the Club door.

The cop was struggling. He didn't know where he was being taken because they had placed a black hood over his face at Snake's. The duct tape remained in place.

"Ah, I see the retrieval process has begun," Snake said, as he eyed the boys trussed to Posts #1&2.

The cop, with difficulty, was placed on Post #3. Tied tightly into place with a full-length of bondage rope.

"Get out of that, boy," snarled Butch as he tied a number of knots in the roping.

The cop's legs were tied tightly to the posts too. "This will take some of the piss out of you."

The cop's chest was heaving. He looked even sexier with his uniform slightly disheveled. His shirt had been partially unbuttoned to reveal a handsome set of nips. His military boots were scuffed.

Once the cop was secured into place, the three Leathermen had to inspect the other candidates.

They nodded in agreement. Snake spoke the obvious, "Good boy material."

The guys cracked open cold beer from the refrigerator. They lighted fresh cigars. They watched from a distance as the cop continued to struggle against his bonds. The other two boys remained fairly quiet.

"Looks like this boy got quite a work out from someone," Mark snorted. The boy's pants were around his knees and there was cum all over him.

"Number #2 doesn't look like he has had any action." said Butch.

He ambled over to the boy and raised the boy's jaw. He looked into the boy's eyes and remarked, "You okay, boy?"

The boy shook his head and mumbled something behind the zippered mouth of the black Leather hood.

"What's that, boy? You want your cock smacked?"

The boy violently shook his head.

Butch got right into the face of the boy and said, "Well, all right, if that's what you want done. I'll be glad to oblige. We want our boys to feel welcome here." He snorted at his own remarks as he retrieved a small cock whip from the wall.

He unzipped the boy's pants. The boy's cock was shrunken. Butch pulled it roughly with his big meaty hands and applied the Leather cock whip to it. Butch enjoyed the flogging and continued his mission, a mission to get the boy's cock hard and full of boyjuice.

The boy's cock responded.

"That's better, boy," Butch said as he began squeezing the boy's cock with his fingerless, studded gloves. After stroking it, he would press the studs into the shaft of the cock. The boy flinched. The studs were like pinpricks into the boy's cockshaft.

"Shit, I should have studs put on the palms too," Butch thought, but he dismissed that notion, "Too hard to ride a cycle with those in place."

He continued to pull on the boy's cock, slapping it with his gloved hand, flogging it, and pressing the spikes from his gloves into the boy's meat.

The boy continued moaning the whole time, although it was muffled through the hood. Butch didn't even notice- he was too engrossed in his own pleasure.

Butch's cock was hard and firm. It strained against his Leather crotch. He pulled his own cock out and began repeating the process of flogging, squeezing, and 'spiking'. He enjoyed it. His cock was lengthening as he continued to play with his cock with one hand and the boy's cock with the other. The boy was apparently not enjoying the process one bit.

After a length of time, Butch ramped up the action. He began squeezing and pulling on the boy's cock, thinking of it as a rubber dildo. The boy moaned even louder, his head rocking from side to side. His arms pulling against the manacles. Butch continued to be too absorbed in his play to notice. He wouldn't have cared any way. His pleasure was the only thing that mattered.

Butch's iron-like grip had an effect and the boy shot a load of cream, all over Butch's gloves.

"Fuck, boy. That's a penalty." He started slapping the boy with the cock whip across the boy's cheeks. The boy's chest, hips, arms were assaulted too. The boy twisted more and more, but could not escape the torture he was being subjected to.

Butch got decided pleasure from the increased whippings. His right hand administered the whippings, his left hand squeezed his own cock.

His temper abated and he continued a prolonged massage of his own dick. He shot a load which landed on the front of the boy's pants.

"Direct hit," he thought and laughed at his own joke.

THE SEVENTH CANDIDATE

Carson, John and Phillippe rode for quite a while. It was a beautiful afternoon and a man in his Leathers with a cycle between his legs was the next best thing to good mansex. They sped along the ribbons of highway connecting the communities surrounding their homebase. They passed a number of cycles out for their afternoon rides.

Carson, in the lead, signaled that he was turning left. It was a road he was unfamiliar with and wanted to explore. It quickly dissolved into a country road with small, well-kept houses and neat lawns dotting it. People were out in their yards, cutting grass, clipping bushes, and relaxing in lawn chairs. The Leathermen nodded or waved to the people. They waved back. As they came to a stop sign, Carson spotted a young man doing yardwork. He was barechested. He signaled the men to pull over to the side of the road. He dismounted and facing away from the young man, asked his two riding buddies, "What do you think?"

The two men eyed the boy through their mirrored sunglasses. They watched the boy for several minutes.

The boy was raking up piles of grass in long sweeps.

"Look at those male nips, sure would like to suck on those for awhile," John said.

Philippe was willing the boy to turn around so he could view the boy's ass. The boy seemed to oblige and Phillippe was not disappointed.

Two firm asscheeks were packed solidly in his faded jeans.

"Fuck, yeah," Phillippe growled. His cock stirred in his Leathers.

"Let's check him out," Carson suggested as they mounted their cycles and cruised slowly past the yard. The boy looked up and waved.

The guys parked their bikes and sauntered back to the fenced-in yard.

They leaned on the fence. "Looks like you got your work cut out for you, Buddy."

The boy leaned on the rake handle, and wiped a bead of sweat from his forehead.

"Sure do. I come once a week to help my grandmother. She lives there," the boy said, pointing his thumb to the modest cottage in back of him.

The Leathermen reviewed the boy. Man, he was cute. Blonde hair, blue eyes, a fine blonde fur covered his arms and chest. A line of fur disappeared into the waist of his pants.

"You guys want a beer? I was about to take a break."

"That sounds like an excellent idea. Riding brings out the sweat in a man," Carson replied as he wiped an imaginary bead of sweat from his forehead.

The boy motioned them to the porch. He opened a cooler and extracted four beers.

"Grandma doesn't allow beer in the house. I have to bring my own. Picked up a six pack on my way here. She provides the cooler," the boy explained.

There were comfortable rocking chairs on the porch and pretty soon, the three men and the boy were seated on the porch.

"Mind if we smoke?" as John extracted his cigar pouch.

"Just don't let Grandma see you and don't let her see me smoking..." the boy grinned as he accepted a proffered cigar.

The Leathermen liked this boy more and more.

Easy going, muscular, handsome. They all eyed his crotch and could see the outline of a cock in his jeans.

"Where are you guys headed?"

"Oh, we're just out for the afternoon."

"Those are damned handsome bikes you have," the boy remarked, taking a deep puff on his cigar.

"You ride?"

"Me, no, never had the money to buy a Harley. Couldn't even afford a Schwinn bicycle," the boy laughed at his own admission. The men joined in.

"Well, let us give you a ride," Carson offered.

"Oh, man I'd love to, but I got to finish her yard." The yard was about two thirds done.

"You got some other rakes?" John offered.

"Well, yeah, they're in the shed. But I can't ask you to do that..." the boy replied.

Phillippe exited the porch and retrieved three rakes. He handed each of the Leathermen one and kept one for himself.

Working alongside the cute barechested boy, the men had the yard raked in no time at all. The grass clippings were gathered and put on Mrs. Henderson's compost pile.

As Phillippe stored the rakes, the boy went inside to tell his grandmother that he was finished and was going to take a spin with some motorcycle buddies.

Mrs. Henderson appeared on the porch, "Much obliged to you. Can I offer you some iced tea?"

"No thank you, Ma'am," Phillippe replied with his French Canadian accent surfacing, "your grandson took care of that."

"He gave you beer, didn't he? I've told him a hundred times not to drink that stuff," she said disapprovingly.

It was then that she noticed the smoldering cigars that the men were puffing on.

"Jacob, are you smoking too? The devil is gonna grab you by the tail," the grandmother admonished.

"Don't worry, Ma'am, we won't let that happen to him," John promised, thinking, "A group of horny Leathermen will take care of it instead." He smiled at her and she relented in her admonishment of the handsome young man.

Jacob climbed the steps to the porch and kissed his grandmother's cheek. "I'll see you next week. I just have to retrieve my shirt" as he headed inside.

The Leathermen surrounded the old lady and shook her hand. It was an odd sight to see. Three men, clad in head-to-toe Leathers, gently shaking the old lady's hand.

"He's my only grandson. And I'm eighty-seven. I might not live to see another grandchild."

"How old is he, Ma'am?"

"He's seventeen." Red flags went off in each of the Leathermen's heads! A minor, fuck!

"No, wait a minute. That's Charlotte, my granddaughter. Jacob is twenty-one. Should have remembered that- he just had a birthday two weeks ago."

The Leathermen looked at each other, making a mental note to check Jacob's age before they did anything to him.

At this point, Jacob reappeared on the porch. He was wearing a tee shirt promoting the Wayward Inn.

The Leathermen all took an inward sigh of relief. The boy retrieved the six-pack, removing the offensive empties from his grandmother's porch.

He kissed her on the cheek once again.

As the Leathermen and the boy headed up the shoulder of the road, they engaged Jacob in conversation.

Seems the boy wasn't quite as innocent as he appeared. He was a dutiful grandson, but he was his own person.

"Looks like you've been to the Wayward Inn," Carson prompted.

"Yeah, spent my twenty-first birthday there in part..." the boy confessed.

"Well, hell, nothing wrong with that," Carson concluded as he slapped the boy on the back.

The boy got on the back of Phillippe's cycle and soon they were speeding along the road.

The boy was holding his head back, catching the air, his blonde hair blowing in the wind.

"Fuck, man, this is awesome," he shouted to Phillippe.

"Hope you like the rest of the journey, boy." Phillippe replied.

After a good half hour or so, the Leathermen retraced their journey. After all, they had left a boy in the woods.

They found the same spot and idled off to the side of the road. The boy climbed off, looking at them expectantly.

"Don't know about you, Jacob, but I gotta take a piss." Carson marched into the woods and the boy followed.

"Yeah, beer has that effect on men, doesn't it?" the boy replied. He started to unzip his jeans when John walked up behind him. Wrapping his arms around the boy, he said, "Let me help you with that."

The boy was caught off guard, but said, "Oh, I've been pissing by myself for years."

"You don't quite understand, boy," Carson said as he extracted his piss-filled cock.

"We like young boys to take our piss."

"What the hell?" the boy said.

He was pushed down to his knees and Carson's cock was in his mouth before the boy could protest the action. Carson's stream of piss coursed down the boy's throat.

Carson's cock was quickly replaced by John's cock, which delivered a full stream too.

As John finished, shaking the dew from his cock, the boy started to get up. Phillippe, with his muscular arms, pushed him down to his knees and said, "Not so fast, one more tap to empty."

As he emptied his cockload of piss into the boy's throat, John hogtied the boy's hands behind him. The boy began struggling and the piss landed all over his face and down his chest.

The boy sputtered after Phillippe had finished, "What the hell is going on?"

The three Leathermen surrounded him and Carson explained, "We're looking for handsome young men to service members of our Club. We think you would be a worthy candidate. You can go willingly or unwillingly." The men tightened the circle around the boy.

The boy looked into the faces of the three men. He looked at their Leathers, their gloved hands, their mirrored sunglasses, their tight Leather pants, the heavy boots on their feet.

"Do I get to wear Leather?"

"Boys earn it, but yes, you eventually wear Leather in the Club."

"Awesome, man. I'm in."

"Good boy," announced Carson as he raised the boy to his feet and slapped him on the back.

The three Leathermen gave him reassuring hugs as they explained that they had to retrieve another boy from a nearby location.

The hitchhiker had lost some of his spirit. He merely stood in place as they approached him. He had been tied to the tree for three or four hours. The men gave him one of the beers, which he gulped down in large gulps.

The willing boy Jacob helped them to re-secure the hitchhiker onto John's bike. The black bandana was tightly tied around the boy's mouth once again. Jacob crawled on the back of Phillippe's bike. Carson was still carrying the hitchhiker's backpack, thinking "he won't need this for awhile." The Leathermen roared back to the Club with two fine candidates.

LET THE GAMES BEGIN

With their mission accomplished, Max, Mick and de Lorenzo loaded their future Leather boys on their cycles. Max rode 'shotgun' just in case any trouble should arise. The boys had gone willingly, of course, but you never knew when a boy might have a change of heart. As a precaution, the boys' hands were tied behind their backs, duct tape over their mouths.

The Leathermen arrived at the Club, finding Snake, Butch and Mark already there. The new detainees were quickly trussed into place at Posts #4&5.

Mick couldn't keep his eyes off Tim, de Lorenzo was having a hard time staying away from that tasty bootblack Joe. Leather lust is a powerful emotion. They had already tasted the handsome boys' abilities and wanted more. Fucking lots more.

They busied themselves with reviewing the other candidates.

"Hey, fuckers, we got a cop," Max announced. He strode over to the cop, his heavy engineer boots sounding like bricks being dropped against the floor.

Max raised the cop's hooded head. The boy's eyes registered contempt and hatred.

"He's got a fire in his belly. He's fucking mad at being here." Mex further declared, "Just the way I like them."

He reached down with his Leathered hands and traced the outline of the boy's cock in his uniform pants.

"Decent," he remarked. He pulled a cigar out of his cycle jacket, chewed off the end, and lighted it with his right hand while still feeling the boy's cock through his pants.

"You got a nice cock, son. I'm going to enjoy playing with it," Max said. He was right up in the cop's face. The cop mumbled something, but he conveniently had duct tape over his mouth.

Max unzipped the boy's uniform pants. The boy's healthy cock was coaxed out with the rough gauntlets that Max wore.

"Well, the cop has a nice cock and with a little coaxing, it will be a real man's cock," Max taunted. The cop shook his head from side to side. The rough gauntlets, with no lube, slid up and down the cop's cock which soon lengthened under the expert guidance of Max's experienced hands. He had handled many cocks in his day.

With the other hand, he pulled his cock out and began massaging it to full length.

When his cock was hard, he unbuttoned the cop's shirt and pinched the boy's nipples. They apparently had never been played with before and the boy flinched as Max's fingers pinched them hard. First the right, then the left. The boy emitted a moan as his tits continued to be manhandled.

Max rubbed the boy's chest with the gauntlets. The gauntlets were more like sandpaper than soft Leather. "But, hell," Max thought, "they'll do the job." Despite the shaking of his head, the cop's cock was lengthening. Max reached down and pulled out the boy's nutsac. Soft and loose, with two low hanging balls residing inside.

Max pulled on them with the rough gauntlets, eliciting another moan from the boy.

Max determined that he needed two more hands, so he called Mick over. Mick was glad to oblige. He wore tight Damascus gloves and began pinching and squeezing the cop's nipples. His grip might not have been as hard as Max's; but it sure as hell had an effect on the cop.

The boy began twisting and moaning as his cock hardened. His balls were being rolled in the big meaty hand of Max, roughened by the gauntlets.

"Atta, boy, now we're getting a reaction from you."

Max began slapping the hardened cock with his gauntlet. Mick twisted on the cop's tits. The cop reared his head back.

"I think we've made contact," Max snorted.

He began slapping the cock harder- it hardened even more, the head enlarging. Max twisted on the cop's balls and then began slapping them too.

Mick continued a steady, unrelenting pressure on the cop's tits. The boy's body was arching forward and backward as the pulling and slapping continued.

Max ended the cock-slapping, but began to squeeze on the shaft of the cock. The head was fully swollen, the shaft throbbing.

"I knew it, his tits are hotwired to his cock," Mick observed, "He'll be one of us in no time."

The rough gauntlet continued to squeeze, slowly rubbing up and down the shaft of the cop's boner. A drop of dew appeared in the piss slit.

Max's cock was fully aroused and he placed it within the palm of his gauntlet, next to the cop's throbbing rod.

He stroked both with a rough ferocity, while still pulling on the boy's nutsac.

Mick's cock was begging for release from his Leathers, but he couldn't abandon his mission at this crucial point.

Max began jerking on the two cocks, with such intensity it felt like he would pull both of them off the bodies to which they were attached.

Max began to moan as he felt his cumjuice rise in his shaft. The boy must have been experiencing the same thing because the piss slit of his cockhead was wide open.

Mick pinched the boy's tits as if his fingers were iron clamps. The boy began breathing heavily as his cock pulsed up and down in Max's hand.

Max yelled, "Shit, I'm gonna shoot. This muthafucker has my cock so fucking hard. I knew a fucking cop was good for something…" His voice trailed off as his cock shot a load, spraying everything in its path. The boy soon shot a load as well, hitting Max's bare chest.

"Fuck!" Max yelled, as he continued to cum.

Mick released the cop's tits from his gloved hands. He pulled out his fully-aroused boner and shot a load, aiming it at the boy's military boots.

A gob of cum settled on the boy's right boot and some landed on his left boot.

The men stood for a few moments, recovering. The boy's cock remained hard for some time. He remained silent but if you could have peered underneath the Leather mask, you would have seen a smile on his face.

As the men recuperated by dragging on cigars, the last two boys were escorted into the Club by Carson, John, and Phillippe.

One struggled, one did not. Both were quickly tied to Posts #6&7. Jacob was hooded like the rest.

"Fuck, isn't that a handsome sight?" Carson remarked. All seven candidates were now in place, awaiting the pleasures of the Club members, "We gotta clean these boys up a little. Hell, it looks like they've been through a war." The boys were variously covered in piss or cum or sweat, or a combination of all three.

Everyone wanted to help as it meant that the boys would be stripped of their clothing- with only their boots in place. Nine Leathermen, seven candidates. Stripping them took no time at all. And soon the boys were standing naked, strapped to Posts #1-7.

The Leathermen stood back, beaming like proud Fathers. They had chosen well.

As they were admiring their handiwork, Rick, Chuck and Jim blustered in. They had headed to the Wayward Inn and kicked back a few beers, shot a couple games of pool, and carried on like the Leathermen they were.

"Hey, men, since we're all here- let's have a brief meeting," Carson announced, "Good work. I think we have chosen well. If these boys prove themselves worthy candidates, we'll have a full complement of subs serving us. As you know, they have to be put through our initiation rites. All of you are expected to be here tonight as well as the next three nights. We'll put the boys through their rites of passage. As you know, that means mouth, cock, piss and ass."

The guys hooted- they didn't have to be reminded of the next few nights of pleasure. They grabbed their crotches in anticipation.

Carson continued, "Now that the boys have been stripped, you are on your honor to observe the rules. Concentrate on the area in question for the night in question. You are not allowed to bring your subs to these nights. Fuck them at home or wherever you ff…"

"I fuck them in the ass," Max shouted. Everyone laughed.

"We know, Max, we know. And you do a damned good job of it!" Carson replied.

"The boys will be in bondage for the four days, but two of us will be appointed as DenMasters to give them water, feed them, escort them to the bathroom…," Carson continued, "That is the only time they will not be in restraints. Hooded at all times. They will be manacled to the workover tables for sleep shifts. The first initiation will begin tonight at 2100 hours"

Carson appointed de Lorenzo and Butch as the DenMasters and they seemed happy with the selection. After all, they could fondle the boys when no one else was around. de Lorenzo was eyeing that cute bootblack while Butch was looking at the handsome physique of the cute young man tied to Post #7. Yes, being a DenMaster was an enviable position. Of course, it meant that you couldn't spend much time at home. Boys had to be supervised.

Every one of the Leathermen wanted to head home and put on their heaviest Leathers for some heavy duty S&M activity. Everyone wanted to retrieve his toys for his own personal workover on the initiates. Tonight, the boys would be reviewed for their suitability utilizing their mouth.

And it conjured up all sorts of activities- bootlicking, cocksucking, rimming, sucking nipples. Not one man departed the meeting without a hardened cock and dirty thoughts swirling through his mind.

ORAL PLEASURES

The Leathermen went home, except for Butch and de Lorenzo.

John and Carson arrived home and immediately went to the dungeon where their two captive boys had spent the day. John unchained one and led him to the bathroom. He fed the boy and gave him water. Carson took charge of the other boy. Both boys were grateful to be released from the fetters they were in- after all, they had been manacled since John and Carson left on their mission in the early morning.

Carson and John led them up to the living room where the Leathermen settled in their comfortable Leather-upholstered wing chairs. The boys were ordered to bring their Masters fresh cigars and a snifter of brandy before kneeling in front of their Sirs. The boys remained attentive to the needs of their Masters, sticking out their willing tongues when the ash lengthened on their cigars.

Carson and John discussed the seven candidates and the likelihood of each boy's success or failure.

"I'm just glad we didn't have to share these boys with the Club," John remarked.

"Well, John, we are going to have to say something, especially if one or two of the candidates don't work."

"There's nothing in our 'Constitution' that says we have to," John countered.

"We formed this Club with a Leatherman's Creed, and we are the President and Vice-President, you know...," Carson replied.

They continued to argue, continued to puff on their cigars. Carson reached over and rubbed the head of the boy who was serving him. The boy's head was still encased in a Leather hood.

John had already pulled his boy's head to his own Leathered crotch. The boy's head, also covered in a black Leather hood, was nuzzling John's crotch with his cheeks and jaw.

"They're such good, obedient boys," John concluded.

"I know," Carson sighed.

Before the cigars were half-finished, the Leatherman's cocks were inserted in the boys' mouths and the men were enjoying an erotic tonguing.

Their cocks stiffened as the boys bathed the hardened shafts and throbbing cockheads with their saliva.

Although the two Leather partners attempted to continue their conversation, they were both aroused by the boys' attention to 'cock duty'.

A precursor of things to come.

Although they prolonged the action as long as they could, their cocks exploded cum into each of the boy's mouths.

"Lick it off, son," Carson ordered, pushing the boy's head onto his cock. John indicated that his boy should do the same. After this had been accomplished, the Leathermen led the boys upstairs. They were manacled in place for their evening's rest. It would be a long night before the two Leathermen returned home.

The partners went to the dressing room. It looked like a Leather shop, with racks of jackets, pants, breeches, chaps, shirts. Rows of boots. A wall of toys.

The men stripped their motorcycle Leathers off and began preparing for the evening. Full harnesses, jockstraps with detachable studded cods.

Tight chaps with military striping down the sides. Shirts with matching striping on the epaulets and pockets. Heavy Langlitz jacket. Dehner boots. Muir Caps. Wrist gauntlets. Tight black Damascus gloves. Gauntlets over those.

They admired each other in the full-length mirror in their dressing room.

"Fuck, John, you look so incredibly handsome. Can I rape you?"

"I was about to say the same thing," John grinned at his partner.

They embraced, with a long, lingering kiss.

They gathered a bag of appropriate toys and climbing aboard their Harleys, left for the night ahead.

Meanwhile, the Club stood ready for the first night of activities. de Lorenzo and Butch had managed to keep their cocks in their pants and had not molested any of the boys. The thought had crossed each other's minds, however! The boys stood strapped to the posts, positions they had been in since the afternoon, with short respites for sleep and bathroom. Most of the boys stood silently, although several of them struggled on occasion. The hitchhiker, Post #6, was particularly restless.

de Lorenzo and Butch were seated at a table, their feet propped up on top. Both were smoking cigars, both were absenty playing with their cocks. Both were in their motorcycle Leathers from the day- of course, as DenMasters, they couldn't leave. "Hell, I ain't in no beauty contest. A little mud, a little dirt, a little piss, and a little cum. That's my idea of 'dressing up'," thought Butch.

de Lorenzo asked Butch, "You get any action today?"

"Sure as hell did. My cock invaded a cop's ass, #3. It was like popping a cherry. That boy had never taken cock up his ass. I bet his hole is pretty sore after three cocks had knocked on his back door." The men hooted at the thought.

"How about you? Did you invite your little Casper out to play?"

"I got a good swabbing- it was fucking awesome. That bootblack Joe from the Wayward Inn went down on my cock. Damn, that boy can excite me! Look at that cute boy, #5. Hell, he needs a big Leatherdaddy to take care of him. And I'd like to take care of him- up the ass, down his throat!" The men's cocks were aroused, but the Club members were due to arrive soon.

"Ah, hell," de Lorenzo said, "what's a little foreplay before the event?"

He went over to the handsome bootblack. The boy's hands were suspended above his head. His body was covered in black fur. He wore heavy engineer boots. His handsome face, of course, was covered with a black Leather hood. A bush of black fur surrounded the handsome meat hanging down between his legs.

de Lorenzo, with his tight Damascus gloves, tweaked the boy's nipple with one hand and squeezed the boy's balls and cock with the other. The boy reacted- a discernible moan was heard through the hood. He mumbled something, but the mouth was zippered shut.

de Lorenzo looked over and realized that Butch had dozed off at the table. "Hell," de Lorenzo, "what he don't know won't hurt the fucker." He unzipped the mouth and thrust his tongue in the boy's mouth. He pulled on the boy's cock and soon, had his cock out too. He manipulated them together until the cocks were hard and throbbing.

The boy's tongue was meeting his tongue. The boy was breathing heavily. de Lorenzo's hands were everywhere at once- caressing the boy's back, his asscheeks, pulling on his tits, pulling on the boy's cock along with his own. de Lorenzo circled the boy's nipples with his fingers, and then pinched them tightly. The boy's body arched backward- enjoying every second. He instinctively knew that it was de Lorenzo. As de Lorenzo continued a frenzied pumping of the two cocks, a hand pulled on his left shoulder and Butch announced, "You fucking idiot! You know you're not supposed to do that."

Momentarily surprised, de Lorenzo pulled his tongue out of the boy's mouth, "I can't fucking help it, I want this boy for my own."

Butch pulled him away from the boy, "Get the hell over there, you son-of-a-bitch. You're not getting me in trouble just for your raging hormones.

You can have him after the other Club members arrive. Now get over there." Butch pushed him toward the table.

They started arguing. Fists were clenched and Butch hit de Lorenzo squarely in the jaw. de Lorenzo stumbled backward, falling over a chair.

"You fucking bastard," de Lorenzo yelled as he got up and made motions to tackle Butch. Fortunately, Max entered the Club at that moment. Sensing what was going on, he stood between the two glowering Leathermen.

"Stop it right now," Max warned.

Curses were thrown, but Max was a big fucker and he stood between them until each had cooled down. The testosterone level in the Club was already rising and it wouldn't be the first conflict as the men vied for the attentions of the fresh meat.

Fortunately, the rest of the guys began to filter in, one more handsome than the next. A sea of black Leather, mounds of cockflesh contained within studded cods. For the most part, every man was in chaps, exposing their handsome asses. Heavy gauntlets covering their hands which were ready to squeeze, fondle, pinch, and explore. Some members were barechested, harnesses outlining their man nips. Others wore full Leather, but the jackets or shirts would soon be discarded. Each man proudly wore a Muir cap.

Carson and John were the last to arrive. Carson banged his Leathered fist on the table.

"Tonight, Leathermen, is the first night of the initiation rites. As you already know, it is a test of the boys' oral abilities. Since there are seven boys, I've put the boys' numbers in my cap. If you draw a number you get to work over the boy first round. If you draw a blank, you'll have a second round opportunity to work over a boy." It seemed a logical, if slightly infantile, way of conducting the session, however, it had worked in previous years.

The drawing began and Max was the first to select. His big meaty cock was already pointing upwards in his studded cod as he drew No #3, the cop. "Hot damn, I've wanted to feel that cop's mouth on my cock since I first viewed him."

In short order, the Leathermen had picked their numbers or blanks and the oral session of the initiation began.

Max repositioned the cop so that he was on his knees. It took some forceful coaxing, but the cop was soon kneeling. Max rubbed his already hardened cod with his rough gauntlets. His cock was throbbing as he unzipped the mouth of the boy's hood.

"Open wide, boy!" he instructed. When the boy resisted, Max pulled the boy's jaw open. Tearing off his cod, he thrust his big dick in the boy's mouth. The boy gagged.

"Take it nice and slow, boy," Max ordered as he began to pump his dick into the boy's mouth.

All the men wanted to try the boys out for cocksucking. Pretty soon, there wasn't an empty boy's mouth in the Club. Some were more experienced than others- the hustlers at Posts No.#1&2 had had plenty of experience and Snake and Mick were the beneficiaries of that experience. Butch took special delight in pushing his meat into the boy's mouth of Post No.#5. de Lorenzo, who had drawn a blank, fumed in the background. Carson, who had also drawn a blank, stood back and observed. The cute little lawn boy at Post No.#7 was doing a damned decent job for being so new at all this. He was envious as he watched Mark work his cock into the boy's throat.

All the boys seemed to perform their newly-found duties well.

Leathered bodies were thrusting and pumping, asses clenching, dicks throbbing.

Leathered hands pulling jaws toward their crotches, holding tightly to boys' shoulders. Heads rearing back as the thrusting became more intense. Sucking. Balls slapping against boy's chins. Leathermen moaning. Instructions of "Take it all, boy. Suck that rod! Fuck my dick with your mouth, boy."

Like fireworks being shot off in rapid succession, the Leathermen started cumming. And cumming. Jism dripped out of the boys' mouth and down the chins of their hoods. The more experienced boys licked the piss slits dry. The Leathermen continued to pump until there was no more cum to pump.

Max was the last man to come. He was able to edge his climax longer than anyone else. Pulling his cock out just at the point of jacking off.

Slapping the boy for not sucking hard enough and then reinserting his cock into the cop's mouth. The cop seemed to enjoy it each time the cock was thrust in his mouth and juiced it up before vacuuming it once again. Even Max couldn't control his cock and shot a huge load of cum. The boy licked the mouth of the hood, gathering every drop of the Leatherman's cum.

The Leathermen relinquished their suckboys to the men who had not had the opportunity of having their bones sucked.

Numbers were once again placed in the cap and the procedure began again for Session #2.

de Lorenzo drew No#1 and reluctantly went over to the first hustler plucked from the alley. His cock was hard, but he was thinking of Joe, the bootblack. He thrust his cock in the boy's mouth and was pleasantly surprised that the boy knew what he was doing. His cock arched upward in the boy's mouth. The boy tongued every inch of de Lorenzo's cock. After all, the boy was an experienced cocksucker. de Lorenzo released his anger and really began to enjoy having his rod worked over by the boy.

He roughly pulled the boy's head toward his cock and soon, the boy had de Lorenzo's meaty balls in his mouth too.

"Fuck, yeah, boy. Good boy," as he began an intense pumping.

Only Boys #2 and #7 were without a man. Both knelt silently. Max, always horny, had himself pleasured by Boy #7.

Finally, Snake sauntered over to Boy #2 and lifted him up to his feet, readjusting the bondage ropes. He thrust his left tit into the boy's mouth. Pushing the boy's head down on the nip, he ordered the boy to suck it. The boy obliged him and Snake's cock arched upward. Snake's glove-covered hand rubbed it, tweaking the head of his cock. With his thumb, he squeezed open the piss hole. Snake's tit, with nipple ring, was being sucked on as if it had a snake bite sucker on it. He ordered the boy to concentrate on his other nip. His cock continued to enlarge. He pressed against the boy's cock which was only momentarily at rest. Snake pressed the boy's head against his nips, alternating between the two. "Fuck, yeah," he thought, as his body arched backward.

The Leathermen in Session #2 were just as horny as the men in Session #1. Hooded heads were pushed down on throbbing rods. Gloved hands were pulling on boys' tits and cocks.

And in a similar climax, the Leathermen shot their loads into the mouths of the willing boys.

After an interlude of time, the men pulled their spent cocks from the boys' mouths.

With all the Leathermen satisfied for the moment, Carson and John went about repositioning the boys for the second phase of the evening. Boot Worship. Each boy was now manacled around the ankles to his Post. The boys were now resting on their bellies.

Most of the men had pulled a cigar from their cases and lighted up.

"Leathermen, listen up," Carson started, "it's time for boot worship. Max, I'd ask that you go in the second session because it's gonna take two boys to lick your boots." The guys laughed easily. Max had worn his crotch-high Wescos. He nodded agreement.

Several of the guys had worn their spit-polished Dehners to complete their uniform look, but some had worn their engineer boots. de Lorenzo and Butch still had on their boots from a dusty day of riding.

Chairs were placed in front of each boy, so that the man having his boots serviced could stretch out. The men brought their favorite paddling device- whether it was a flogger or a paddle to discipline the boy in case he missed a spot.

Numbers were arranged in the hat and selections were made.

Phillippe chose first and was to be serviced by Joe, the bootblack. Joe stretched his naked body out on the floor. He was muscular with a particularly handsome muscular ass. He was incredibly seductive as he lay on the floor, a Leather hood covering his features, except his tongue which he flicked in and out.

Phillippe sat in the designated chair. He pressed his Dehners into the boy's right shoulder. The boy lifted it gently and began to lick the heel.

His tongue took long swathes around the toe of the boot. Phillippe could feel the boy's tongue through the supple Leather of his boot. It felt so fucking erotic. Phillippe was aroused by the boy's tonguing, pulling out his own cock and playing with it. Despite viewing the man's cock, Joe did not deviate from his task. He began licking up the shaft of the black Leather boot, massaging the calf with his tongue. Phillippe began to twitch his legs, it felt so good. The boy continued to tongue the

Master's boots as if they were the finest chocolates. As the boy came closer to the top of the boot, Phillippe swatted him with a riding crop.

"Boy, you missed a spot, below the buckle. to the left of the buckle. Redo it, NOW!"

Joe obliged, but both knew that there really was no spot. Phillippe just enjoyed the tonguing.

Joe increased the intensity of his stroking and licking with his tongue. His hands massaged the calves of the boot. He had strong, powerful hands, from all the boots he had polished. His sexy pink nipples showed through the black fur covering his chest.

Phillippe's cock hardened even more, viewing those nips. He couldn't wait for nipple play. He reached down and pinched them with his hands covered in Damascus gloves. They became firm and hard with Phillippe's fingers squeezing them. Despite that, the bootblack continued the massaging of the man's booted legs.

Phillippe was hard. The boy asked permission to approach his Sir's cock. When given permission, he reached up and began stroking the Leatherman's cock. He rubbed it with his powerful hands. And without warning, Phillippe shot. The boy quickly collected the cum in his bare hands. He spoke, only saying, "Sir, may I taste your cum?" He cocked his hooded head to one side.

"Yes, boy. Lick it up," Phillippe answered the question. The boy greedily tongued it from his own hands. He cleaned them thoroughly before finishing his bootlicking.

"Good boy. Good boy." Phillippe said.

Other Leathermen's boots were almost finished in their worship by the boys. Every boy had done well, but Joe had Phillippe's vote as the best bootlicker.

Session #2 of bootlicking began with a change of Leathermen. The boys seemed anxious to continue.

Max, by virtue of his hunky Wescos, got the pleasure of having two boys service his boots. Tim was the slender lad captured at the Leather store. Jacob was the young fellow raking his grandmother's lawn when he was picked up. The boys had to be repositioned so that they were manacled next to one another. Max stretched out his Wescos so that the toes were comfortably situated under the boys' chests. He had lighted a big fucker of a cigar and was puffing on it when the boys began massaging his boots with their tongues. Both boys were enjoying the scene and were doing well. Jacob was servicing the left boot, Tim was servicing the right.

Jacob was very inexperienced. Max went easy on him at first, but his sadistic qualities surfaced and he began lashing the boy across the back when he missed a spot- the boots were dirty from Max's many adventures. Tim was a better bootslave, but, of course, he got lashed too. Max liked to hear the crack of the Leather across a naked boy's back and ass.

The boys tongued slowly up the ankle to the shaft of the boot. Max could feel the boys' tongues through the Leather. It was fucking erotic. He began fingering his cock through his cod. The cock was leaking cum at this early stage. The boys continued licking and as they tongued up the shaft, it became necessary for them to lean their naked chests against the lower part of the boot. Max viewed young male flesh stretched across his boot. The muscles in their backs flexing. Their ass muscles expanding and contracting as they licked his boots clean.

He occasionally flogged those handsome backs and asses even though he would rather be shoving his cock up one of those asses.

Tim began the difficult task of cleaning the tongue of the boot. He could have untied the laces, but he chose to flick his tongue in between the laces. Jacob viewed this action out of the corner of his eye, and followed suit.

Max was puffing on his cigar, enjoying two naked boys rubbing on his boots with their hands, their naked chests, and he envisioned their cocks rubbing against the black Leather boots. He envisioned the toe of his boot playing with the tip of their cocks, arousing each one.

He smiled. There was nothing better than a handsome, naked boy servicing you.

His cock throbbed as the boys' willing mouths came closer and closer to the top of the boot. It was a foregone conclusion that the boys would suck his rod. He pulled his handsome dick out of his codpiece. Tim flicked the tip of the piss slit as he finished the top of the right boot. Jacob was a little slower, but soon was doing the same. The boys alternated in swabbing the cockhead.

Max thought he would jack at any minute. Both boys' heads were now concentrating on his cock. Jacob began licking the shaft, Tim caught the Leatherman's balls in his mouth and rolled them over his tongue.

"Fuck!" Max said loudly, as he arched up out of the chair. The boys continued for some time, but Max couldn't control the on-off switch of his cock any longer and shot. Spraying the boys in their hooded faces. He wiped it off the hoods and fed it to the willing boys.

"Good boys. Good boys," Max concluded as he rubbed the boy's hooded heads.

Several of the Leathermen wanted to be rimmed, testing the boys in yet another service. They had worn chaps for easy access to their holes.

In a switch from the normal procedure, Carson asked for the boys to volunteer. The hitchhiker raised his head and was quickly paired off with Mick.

Mick loved to have his ass massaged with a willing tongue. And the hitchhiker, who had been the most problematic of the boys, suddenly was the most willing.

The boy was tied to the post with his hands behind his back. Kneeling. Mick presented his ass to the boy and the boy began a vigorous tonguing of Mick's asshole.

"This boy has real talent," Mick mused as the tongue swabbed as deep as the boy could reach. Mick backed up and the tongue seemed to extend even further.

Mick had pulled his cock out and was rubbing it in rhythm with the boy's tonguing. Mick's ass was moist from the tonguing and his cock was moist from the precum that appeared in the piss slit. The boy's tongue seemed to harden and felt like a small, thrusting cock. He thrust in and out, in and out.

Mick continued to rub his dick with his gloved hands. Mick reached around with his right hand and pushed the boy's face in between his asscheeks. That tongue was flicking in and out.

Mick couldn't control his cockjuices any longer and shot all over the floor of the Clubhouse. He was breathing heavily as the boy continued. He finally pulled away from the boy and remarked, "Excellent, boy. That felt so damned fine. You can clean my ass anytime."

"Thank you, Sir. It would be an honor, Sir," the boy answered.

The night was winding down. The boys were probably exhausted after all the services they had provided. They were given food and water and escorted to the bathroom. They were then led to sleeping accommodations where they were shackled into place. The Leathermen stood around and compared notes. The Club was thick with smoke and the smell of sweaty Leather and drying cum.

Carson concluded the evening. He appointed Mark and Phillippe as DenMasters for the night, both of whom agreed willingly.

The Leathermen left the Club, going back to their own Leather Dens for some rest before tomorrow night's activities.

"As you know, Leathermen, tomorrow night is cock night. Bring your toys. Work those boys' cocks over with whatever you got."

     Sadistic minds went into overload as they thought of all the many pleasures you can have playing with a willing boy's cock.

COCK PLEASURES

The Leathermen mounted their cycles and headed for their own Leather dens, where some of them, just like Carson and John, had submissive boys waiting for them. There wasn't a Leathermen that night who had not gotten his fair share of hot sex, but most of the guys wanted more.

Uniformly, bikers are a separate breed of men, relishing their individuality and freedom. Fuck you, if you don't agree with him. Taking what they want, especially when it comes to the ass of a submissive boy. Although like most Leather bears, they are fairly quiet men unless provoked.

Chuck and Jim were two of those quiet men. Not bold and beefy like Max or Snake. "Just average," they would both say about themselves. But under their Leather jackets beat the hearts of two dedicated Leathermen. They lived in the same block and had often played with one another or worked over a boy together. Jim had acquired the services of a sub last year. He was a good boy. Tall and lanky, brown hair, brown eyes. His name was Beau, of French extraction from Canada. He had served Jim well.

Before the guys left the Club, Jim invited Chuck over for a drink and some extended Leather play. It was hard to turn it off once the testosterone was pumping.

Chuck followed Jim on his cycle and parked it in his own alleyway. He walked the few steps to Jim's house.

The Leathermen climbed up the steps and entered the house.

Chuck followed Jim downstairs to the dungeon where they found the boy obediently waiting. Naked. Much like the candidates, he was manacled into place on a St. Andrew's cross, facing the wall. The boy's hooded head turned instinctively toward the dungeon door as he heard his Master's boots coming down the steps.

"What a nice looking boy, Jim." Chuck remarked as he sidled over and slapped the boy's ass.

Jim picked up a butt paddle and shook his head in agreement.

"How ya doing, boy? You ready for Daddy's punishment?" Jim asked the boy as he unzipped the hood's zipper at the mouth.

"Yes, Sir. Thank you, Sir."

Jim let loose with a paddling of twenty rotations. The boy's ass reddened very quickly, but he did not flinch. He had been trained well.

Handing the paddle to Chuck, Chuck proceeded to paddle the boy twenty times. He rubbed the boy's asscheeks afterward. The black Leather gloves felt so good to the boy. His head arched backward and his back muscles flexed. His long, wiry arms flexed as well.

Next, Jim pulled his favorite flogger off of his belt and flogged the boy, making sure he made contact with the boy's shoulders, arms, back and ass. He silently counted forty rotations.

Now the boy's back was covered in reddening marks. Chuck echoed Jim's flogging rotation.

And so, the evening progressed. The floggings and paddlings increased in intensity, but Jim had worked this boy up to a heightened threshold of pain. He could take several hundred floggings without flinching. Jim wanted to carry him beyond that high mark. Chuck was more than willing to oblige in helping Jim reach that destination.

The boy's ass was now painfully red, and lash marks were beginning to bring blood to the surface. The Leathermen concentrated on the boy's upper back, the area between the boy's shoulder blades. And while the boy's muscled arms flexed against the chains and Leather restraints, he never uttered a moan.

As Chuck continued to work over the boy, Jim stood back and lighted a cigar which he withdrew from his cycle jacket pocket. He marched over to the boy and blew smoke in the boy's mouth. The boy held it in his mouth until he was told to release it.

"Thank you, Sir," the boy replied.

"New trick, I see," Chuck commented.

"Yep, we've been working on ashtray service and breath control," Jim replied.

As Chuck finished his flogging rotation, he stood back and admired his work. The boy's back was crisscrossed with bloody marks.

"Good boy," Chuck told the boy as he rubbed the boy's back with his soft, black Leather gloves.

"Thank you, Sir," the boy answered.

Jim retrieved an inflatable dildo and greasing it with lube, inserted it in the boy's handsome ass.

"Keep it in there, boy," Jim warned as the boy's cheeks clenched shut on the substitute cock. The boy silently hoped that it would be his Master's dick soon.

The boy stood silently as Chuck stood back and lighted a cigar, retrieved from his cigar case.

"Let's leave him for awhile. See if he can hold onto that dildo," Jim suggested as the two Leathermen marched upstairs.

The Leathermen settled into the den and reviewed the Club's candidates.

"A good crop. I want to see some more action from the two hustlers that we picked up. But they seem to be reasonable."

"Yep, I think they'll all turn into good subs for the Club. You taken a shine to anyone yet?" asked Jim.

Chuck hesitated for a moment, reviewing the candidates in his head. "Yeah," he finally replied, "I've taken a shine to No. #7. There's something about him- he looks innocent. And I just like to break in innocent boys."

"He is. Carson, John and Phillippe found him raking leaves in his granny's yard."

"Hell, no," Chuck replied.

"Yep, got right into it. They took him in the woods, tied him up and he was more than eager to take their piss. He would have sucked them off too if they hadn't had to return to the Club."

"I got to test that boy out for myself."

The Leathermen went back to the dungeon. Beau was standing silently with the dildo in place.

"Good boy," Jim told the boy as he slapped the boy's asscheeks. Momentarily caught off guard, the dildo slipped out of place.

Ordinarily that would have been an infraction, but Jim was eager to stick his rod up the boy's hole. He greased it up and slid his cock into place. The boy's asscheeks flexed as they certainly wanted to hold his Master's cock. The boy's handsome butt flexed, as the cock continued its journey into the dark recesses of the boy's ass.

Chuck hovered nearby. "You think he could take two?" he questioned.

Jim inched over and fingered the boy's hole. "Try it."

Chuck greased up his glove and pressed his fingers into the boy's ass. There seemed to be enough room. He was slightly taller than Jim and so, he eased his cockhead into the boy's ass. Damn, if it didn't slide right in, on top of Jim's cock. The boy, for the first time, began moaning. His buttcheeks expanded and contracted as the cocks slid up his asshole.

"Fuck," Chuck moaned as his ramrod crawled up the boy's chute. Jim continued to pump his cock. Jim could feel Chuck's veined cock laying on top of his.

The two Leathermen began pumping harder and harder as the boy's ass took both cocks. Jim was rubbing Chuck's Leathered asscheeks and Chuck was rubbing Jim's.

They continued to pump, their cocks hardened and pulsing within the warm confines of the boy's ass.

Chuck could feel Jim's cock tickling the underside of his cock. The boy was moaning as the men's ramrods throbbed with the intensity of jism inching its way toward release.

The Leathermen continued fondling each other's asscheeks. The boy's arms were straining against the manacles.

Chuck began moaning as he said in ragged breaths, "I'm going to cum! I'm going to… shoot! AAAHHH!" He shot a load followed in close succession with Jim's load.

The boy's head was leaning against the wall. He was breathing heavily too. Jim was gasping for air.

"Damn, that was the best fuck!!" he finally concluded.

The Leathermen pulled their spent cocks out of the boy's receptacle and swabbed the cum off of each other's manrods. They fed it to one another, giving the boy a taste of the combined cumjuices.

"Thank you, Sirs," the boy replied.

The Leathermen reconvened at the Club at 2100 hours. As usual, the men were in full Leathers, ready for some cock pleasures and more to the point, cock pleasuring.

Carson and John had arrived earlier in the evening and had brought a fresh supply of beer. A full box of cigars had been donated by Carson and John from their private humidor. The boys had been brought from the sleeping area and remanacled to the posts. They, of course, were fettered face forward for cock and ball play.

Most men had worn their heavy Leather gauntlets for squeezing, rubbing, twisting, and pulling. Most of the guys had their tight Damascus gloves on underneath for later play.

Carson announced the beginning of the session for this evening and had the usual numbered slips of paper, numbered one through seven, and five blank slips. He tossed them in his Muir cap.

John was to draw first and picked No.#4, the little boy from the Leather shop. The boy was slim, but had a nice, long dick and a loose ball sac.

John went over to his prey and began immediately to squeeze the boy's nutsac. He placed a vacuum pump on the boy's slender cock which soon enlarged with the help of the pump. John continued to roll the nutsac in his gloved hand. The boy was moaning. His cock was hardening in the vacuum tube. John removed the cock from the vacuum pump and squeezed the boy's dick between his two Leathered legs. He could feel the boy's cock throbbing, its head arching toward the crease of John's buttcheeks. His own cock was fully extended in his cod. He released his cock and it settled on top of the shaft of the boy's cock. He began a slow massage of the two cockshafts, backing up so that the boy's cockhead was just touching the legs of his Leather pants. John continued the massage.

John then reversed the two cocks so that his cock was on the bottom, pressing into the loose ballsac of the boy.

Both cocks were hardened. His cock was pressing further and further into the top of the ballsac. The boy's cock was being squeezed in between John's Leathered legs. John rubbed against it, squeezed it. Rubbed his Leather gauntlets along the shafts of both cocks.

The boy was breathing heavily, attempting to contain his cockjuices.

John added pressure to the cock's head with his legs. He increased the rubbing back and forth of the shafts. His own cock's head was enjoying its sequestered time in the loose skin of the ballsac.

John pulled the shoulders of the boy toward him. It increased the area of the boy's cock that was now being squeezed by the muscular legs of the Leatherman. The boy was arching backward as his cock thrust forward and as he felt the pressure of John's cock on the underside of his own cock.

John was beginning to moan as his cock's head opened and shot a load of jism, lubricating the boy's balls and underside of his cock. The boy could not control his cum any longer, seeking permission to shoot. The mouth of his hood was zippered shut, but John knew what the request was.

"Yes, boy, shoot." The boy shot his cum between the clenched legs of the Leatherman. John could feel the muscular thrusts of the cock as it shot.

Repositioning the boy to his knees, he stood with his crotch over the boy's head and made him lick the cum off of his Master's cock. The boy tongued it for some time before John approved of his work. The boy had a good tongue and it felt good. John didn't want the boy to stop so he ordered the boy to lick the cum off his Leathered thighs. The boy did that with little prompting.

Snake had a pair of pinprick gauntlets which added a little spice to his sessions with boys. Snake drew No.#6, the hitchhiker, who had proved to be a good bootlicker. Snake approached the boy and wrapped his pinprick gloves around the shaft of the boy's cock. The boy flinched as the pinpricks dug into his cockflesh.

Once he got beyond the initial reaction, the hitchhiker responded. His cock arched upward, becoming a hardened rod almost immediately.

Snake pulled on the cock. He was able to put both hands, end for end, covering the cockshaft. The pinpricks dug into the boy's shaft. Once the boy's cock was fully aroused, Snake cupped the boy's balls in his left gloved hand. Once again, the boy flinched. Snake rolled the balls in the palm of his hand, making sure every inch of the ballsac was pricked. He cupped the balls and began squeezing them, hard.

The boy pulled backward and Snake pulled the balls toward him. The boy's head reared, wincing in unexpected pain.

Snake ignored the boy's reaction. He was too concentrative on the cock and ball torture. His right hand never stopped pressing the pinpricks into the cockshaft. The pricks were digging in with a delicious sting.

The boy was moaning, shaking his head from side to side. The pain was unabated as Snake rubbed the cockshaft with the pinprick gloves. Fuck, it felt great. Snake's cock was fully tumescent in his codpiece. The codpiece had the same pinpricks inside it, firmly pressing on Snake's own cockflesh. As the cock hardened, the pricks bit into his flesh too.

He continued to squeeze on the boy's nuts and his cock.

Snake was smoking a cigar and blew smoke in the boy's face. He hissed, "Take it like a willing boy. Enjoy it. Enjoy your Leatherman's pleasure through pain, boy."

The boy's arms were pulling against his shackles. It only brought out Snake's sadistic side which caused him to squeeze even tighter. The cock and ballsac were now marked with tiny red dots. He pulled on both. The boy's body moved forward as far as the manacles would allow. The balls and cock were pulled further and further away from his body. Despite the pain, the boy's cock was throbbing with an intensity. Snake's cock was relishing the pricks on it and was fully engorged with cum.

The boy's cock was arched upward, the head fully loaded with cum too. It was only a matter of time before there would be the release of cum from both cocks.

Snake knew it was near climax and squeezed hard, pulling the spiked gloves toward him, toward the boy's cockhead. With that the boy's cock exploded and cum shot all over Snake's cod. Snake continued to squeeze on the nutsac and the boy's dick until it became limp in his hand.

It was then that he said, "Good boy." He remanacled the boy and ordered the boy to lick the cum off his cod. The boy could feel the pulsing rod inside Snake's cod.

After the boy licked the cod clean, Snake unsnapped the cod and made the boy suck his manrod. Since he was so close to climax, it was only a matter of minutes before he shot cum down the boy's throat. After the boy licked the cock clean of its cum, Snake patted the boy on his hooded head and released him from his duties.

Rick waited patiently during Session #1. He had drawn a blank in Session #1. His bag of toys was dropped near his booted feet as he absently sucked on a beer, alternating it with a fresh cigar. He had just gotten some new toys from his favorite 'toy' store and was anxious to try them out on a captive boy. Finally, all the Leathermen relinquished their 'posts' and numbers were drawn. Rick selected a slip of paper which read No. #2. One of the hustlers. Guy with a cycle jacket on when they first met. Resisted their proposal. All three Leathermen had pissed on him but Rick had not really had the chance to test him out. Rick was one of the men without a submissive boy. Now was the time to find a suitable candidate. Let the games begin.

He marched over to Boy #2. He lifted the boy's hooded head. "Playtime, boy."

The boy just looked dully at him. The boy had seemed to rally for the sporting event held the night before and Rick hadn't heard any complaints from Carson who had just finished playing with him.

Rick dropped his bag of toys near his booted feet and grabbed the boy's cock and balls in his hands which were covered with soft, buttery Leather gauntlets. Despite any reservations the boy had, his cock began to respond.

Rick pulled out some run-of-the-mill clothespins, swiped from his grandmother's clothesline when clotheslines still existed. Rick was a precocious sadist, first putting them on his nipples when he was just twelve.

"Ricky, tell me what you want to be when you grow up?", his grandmother had once asked.

Well, he didn't tell her he wanted to be a sadist to be sure! But that's what he had grown up to be. And he really enjoyed the initiation rites administered by the Club. The boy he had last year had not worked out and had asked for release. Rick was disappointed, but it wasn't a good match and had let him go. Rick was always up for more Leather play. More homomasculine play. More sadistic play.

Rick began placing the clothespins in an arch from the boy's nipples down his ribcage to his hips. They really didn't hurt- not until big Daddy decided to pull them off.

He then pulled out a mean-looking vise. A ball-crusher. Squeeze those boy balls. Cock too.

As the boy began to feel the pressure of the vise, he winced and pulled from side to side. Rick slapped him sharply on the cheek.

"Stand still, boy," he ordered.

The boy momentarily complied, but as Rick applied more pressure the boy began to wrench his arms, attempting to kick his shackled feet.

"I said, Stand still, asshole!" Rick ordered in a more strident tone.

He eased the pressure off the vise a little, conceding, "Okay, I'll let you get used to it."

He rubbed the cockhead with his gauntlets. He fondled the balls with them as well. The boy relaxed visibly.

Rick leaned into the boy's hooded face, "This ain't no massage parlor, boy. Now get used to it."

Rick pulled out a length of fine bondage rope and wrapped it around the base of the cock and balls. He tied it around the boy's waist. He tightened it so that the vise was now sticking straight out. The boy's cock was pointing straight ahead.

He then attached a pair of mean nip fuckers to the boy's tits. The boy once again winced. The tit clamps were connected to a chain. With a short length of rope, Rick attached the nip chain to the vise. Any pull on the cock would send a sadistic message to the boy's nips and vice versa.

He began rubbing the boy's chest, occasionally tweaking the nip clamps with his Leathered hands. The boy flinched every time. Rick enjoyed seeing the reactions on a boy's face. Shame his face was hooded.

Rick alternated, rubbing the nips and then pulling on the chain. Pinching the clothespins. Slowly ramping up the pressure of the vise on the boy's cock and balls. Watching the boy's cockhead as it became swollen with cum.

Rick pulled out a mean little fucker- a flogger with metal tips. He began a slow flogging of the boy's chest, purposely catching the chain of the nip clamps. All in one motion, sending a message to the boy's nips, cock and balls.

Rick's cock was getting excited in its Leather cod. He would absently rub it between rotations of the flogger.

Twisting the screws on the vise. Adding pressure to the nips with small lead weights suspended from the clamps. Squeezing on the clothespins. Rick was a Master at this type of sadistic pleasure. He wanted to prolong it. He could go all fucking night. As men finished their session with their respective boys, they came to watch.

Rick enjoyed it. He was an exhibitionist and was proud to show his handiwork with a willing boy as his subject. The boy had calmed down and was moaning softly, but he was no longer twisting and flinching. The threshold of pain had been stepped over and the boy was embracing it as a mature slaveboy should.

Rick continued while the guys watched. The vise was tightened. The rope was pulled to make sure everything was taut. The tits were being pulled with the clamps and the weights. The boy's dick was hard and juicy within its' closure. The balls were full and hard too. Rick continued his flogging with the metal-tipped flogger. His cock was hardened and throbbing within the cod. The cod was tented and the outline of his big manrod was visible.

He stopped only briefly to flick the ash of his cigar into the boy's mouth. He zipped the mouth hole closed after the boy had tongued the ash.

He continued flogging. Flicking the boy's weighted tits with the flogger. Flogging the head of the boy's cock. The boy's hardened balls.

He began pulling more vigorously on the boy's nips. The boy was groaning more loudly.

He tightened the vise one more crank, crushing the boy's cock and balls in between. A drop of pre cum appeared in the boy's piss slit.

Rick knew that he could not take this boy much further before the boy's cock spewed forth its cum.

He began a frenzied flogging with the mean little fucker, lashing out and catching the boy's molested nips, pulling on the chain that connected them. He fingered the cockhead with his Leather gauntlet. He rubbed the balls which were hard and reddened from the pressure.

He pulled on the titchain with his right hand, holding it straight out, pulling on it. With his left hand, he began pulling the clothespins off the boy's body, not bothering to squeeze them open. The boy was now screaming into the confines of the Leather hood as the clothespins were ripped off of his body. One by one. Despite the pain, the boy's cock was throbbing. As the final clothespin was pulled off, the boy's cock shot a stream of cum, landing on the floor. The boy was screaming, but it had turned into a moment of ecstasy.

In a final action, Rick released the boy's nips from the titclamps. The tits throbbed as blood rushed back into them. Finally, Rick reached down and unscrewed the vise which had held the boy's cock and balls captive. The boy's cock shot some more trapped cum, this time landing on Rick's gauntlet.

Rick held it in front of the boy's mouth until the boy reluctantly licked it off the glove.

Rick announced to the crowd, "Well, this boy has just christened my new toy. I think I've found my boy."

That announcement remained to be seen. Carson announced that it was the end of the evening and appointed Snake and Mick as the DenMasters for the night after reminding that tomorrow night was a glorified piss party. "Drink lots of beer, guys. Come with a full tap."

THE PLEASURES OF PISSING

The Leathermen headed out into the night. A group of them were just too oversexed to go straight home. They rode to the Wayward Inn.

It was late when they arrived and the bar was crowded. The parking lot was filled with lots of bikes. The chrome glistened in the neon light of the Inn's sign.

The men trooped in. It certainly grabbed the attention of the guys there. Men, dressed in the standard uniform of a black Leather jacket and jeans, in every corner of the bar. If truth be told, there probably wasn't a soft cock in the place unless someone had just gotten serviced in the back alley. The guys hustled up to the bar to order their drinks and broke off from the group as they spotted familiar faces or fresh meat.

Butch was one of the guys who journeyed to the bar. Butch was horny. But Butch was always horny. Butch was in his thirties- good-looking, with sandy hair, a well-trimmed beard, and a decent build. He had grown up with five sisters and was the youngest. At an early age, he was teased for being 'one of the girls'. Instead of taking it, he had fought back. He was constantly in trouble in school, getting into fights. It was in high school that he joined the wrestling team and then the football team. He bulked up in high school, enough to earn him a place on defense. He took all his aggressions out on the opposing team, giving at least one poor guy a concussion. He had joined the Army right out of high school, but decided it wasn't for him. "Don't Ask, Don't Tell" was just too much of a temptation and he coupled with two similarly-minded men before realizing he didn't want to hide his orientation. He wanted to fuck men. No two ways about it. He had drifted into several 'careers' and had finally found satisfying work working for a landscaper. He was an outdoors man- he enjoyed getting his hands dirty. It was a natural fit. He had been doing it for about twelve years. He was able to buy his Harley and went off on long weekends when he wasn't called into work. He had several liaisons with men, but none of the relationships had lasted that long. Still, there was that eternal quest.

Butch retrieved his beer and found a place to stand. His eyes drifted over the crowd. "Damn, so many handsome men!", he thought.

He sucked on his beer, stoked his cigar, and just enjoyed watching the guys filter past. He got more than a few cruises. He was in full Leather and made quite an impression.

Butch looked over to the bar. A new contingent of bikers had arrived. All Leathermen- some with chains on their epaulets, others with metal cockrings on the epaulet. Most wore their 'jewelry' on the left indicating that they were tops. One or two wore it on the right. One guy stood out- it was as if a beacon of light was spotlighting him. He stood in the midst of the newly-arrived bikers. Stocky. Shaved bald, but with a big handlebar-type mustache. "I'll just bet he's a hairy one," thought Butch. The guy was dressed in a cop uniform out of Leather. Brown shirt with tan epaulets and cuffs. A bit of a beer belly. Tan pants with brown stripes down the legs. Brown, not black, officer's boots buckled at the knee. Brown gloves.

Butch had to restrain himself from drooling. His cock was leaking cum.

"Fuck," he silently questioned, "is he with someone? Just can't see." He repositioned himself to take a better look. The guy was still surrounded by the group of guys he came in with.

Butch thought, "Hell, he's probably happily partnered."

As the guy took a swig from his beer bottle, his arm flexed. Nice, bulging muscle. "Wonder if there's another bulging muscle?" Butch said under his breath.

"Yes, he has got a considerable cock," a voice said.

"Oh?" Butch replied, trying to sound nonchalantly about it. "Fuck," he thought to himself, "This guy is really hot."

He turned to find a handsome Leatherman standing next to him, swigging his beer. "Yes, that's Michael. He's a cop in real life, but he's one hundred percent Leatherman outside of the 'office'."

"He's very handsome," Butch replied.

"Don't I know it? I have been after him for years. Never succeeded in catching him," the guy said.

"I'm Butch."

"I'm Cal. Nice to meet you."

"He probably has a whole host of boys surrounding him," Butch answered, afraid to hear the truth.

"No, you got him all wrong. He's a bottom. Tie him up and fuck him. That's what he likes." Cal assured Butch.

"No shit?" Butch said, unable to believe that the guy was submissive to anyone.

"No shit, bro."

The crowd of newly-arrived bikers had disseminated and were now doing the cruise, seeking out friends and looking for fresh hook-ups.

Butch knew what he wanted.

He kept his eye on Michael as the Leatherboy circulated. He lost sight of him once again. Butch went over to the bar to retrieve a second beer.

He turned around and Michael was standing right behind him.

"Hey, handsome. Mind if I stand where you're standing so I can order another beer?" Michael said. Butch's tongue practically fell out of his mouth as he replied, "Let me get it for you."

Michael thanked him and handed Butch the empty beer bottle.

Pretty soon, Butch had both bottles in his hand, but instead of handing it to Michael, he clung tightly to it.

"I was headed out to the patio. Want to join me?" Butch said in a hopeful tone.

"Sure, hell of a lot of guys here tonight," Michael observed.

"It's witching hour..." Butch explained. It was indeed almost two o'clock when the bar closed. He would have to move fast if he wanted to bed this guy tonight.

They retired to the patio, where a large contingent of guys were lighting up. Most guys were huddled in groups of two or three.

Butch propped his foot on a flower pot and handed Michael the beer.

Michael nodded his head as a thank you.

"Great night for Leather, isn't it?" Butch observed. It was true, the night was mild and balmy. A gentle breeze blew through the patio area.

"Well, any night is a great night for Leather," Michael offered.

"You ride?" Butch asked

"A Harley- nothing better. I ride at work too- a BMW," Michael replied.

"Oh? What do you do?" Butch asked innocently as if he hadn't any prior knowledge.

"I saw you talking to Cal. I'm sure he told you I'm a cop," Michael stated as a smile appeared on his face. When he smiled, his eyes lighted up. Some crinkles appeared around the eyes, indicating that he was probably older than Butch.

"Okay, I confess, he did fill me in. I asked him who the handsome guy was and he told me."

"So, what else did he tell you?" Michael asked in a leading way.

"Well," Butch answered, "he told me that you were dying to meet me and that you wanted to go home with me for Leather play…"

"Hmmm? Is that right? Hmmm? A very interesting proposal which has merit." Michael replied as his eyes continued to twinkle.

Butch pulled Michael toward him and they engaged in a very long, passionate kiss. Both had their eyes closed and so didn't notice that the lights had been flicked on and off, indicating that the bar was closing.

Guys started filtering toward the exit. Butch instinctively grabbed Michael's hand and escorted him to the exit.

"Where's your cycle?" Butch questioned.

"Over there." His Harley was a low rider, customized. Chrome exhaust pipes. Evil-looking handlebars. Fucking hot. Just like the man who rode it.

"Follow me," Butch ordered as he mounted his cycle. He sped off toward the parkway which took lesser time to get home. He prayed that Michael and his bike would remain close behind and not peel off at a convenient exit.

Butch lived out in the suburbs. A comfortable ranch house with a dungeon in the basement. Handsomely landscaped, of course. Butch had plans of sharing part of the landscape with Michael.

It took them about twenty minutes to arrive at Butch's house. Instead of inviting Michael in, he instructed the boy to wait near the garage. "I'll be right back."

Butch went inside and retrieved bondage rope and a few other toys, as well as a flashlight.

"Follow me," Butch ordered. The cop obediently followed.

They proceeded to a corner of Butch's property, far from the road, far from neighbors.

A sturdy walnut tree was his destination.

"Stand with your arms hugging it, boy." Butch ordered.

Butch quickly tied roping around the boy's wrists. He wound it around the boy's waist, down one leg, up the other leg and tied it off around the boy's waist. The boy was not going anywhere.

Although the boy was tightly trussed to the tree, Butch managed to open the boy's shirt and loosen the boy's belt and pants.

He stood with his body against the back of the boy, his cod pressed tightly into the Leather skins covering the boy's ass. He reached underneath the boy's arms and rolled the boy's tits in his gloved fingers. The boy arched his head upward. Feeling pleasure already.

Butch's cod pressed into the boy's ass crease. As he continued to thrust his cod in the crease, he slowly lowered the boy's uniform pants. A handsome ass greeted him, highlighted by a shafting of moonlight.

As the pants dropped to the boy's knees, Butch continued to roll the tits between his fingers. His cock was enlarging rapidly as he continued to pump his cod into the crack. The boy's naked ass began to follow the rhythm of Butch's pumping.

When his cock was fully aroused, Butch unsnapped his cod. His cock sprang forward. He spit on it for lubrication and eased it up the cop's hole.

The cop moaned, opening his ass for the receipt of the Leatherman's cock.

Butch continued to twist and pull on the cop's tits. They were definitely hotwired to the cop's cock. It was arching upward against the tree.

Butch's cock explored the cop's cave. Inching further and further as Butch encouraged it to do so by thrusting it more violently. The cop was moaning. He began talking, "Oh, yeah, Leatherman, fuck me. I want to take your cock all the way up my hole. Fuck, it feels so good. Fuck, yeah. Fuck me over and over again. Twist my tits. Pull on them. After you fuck me, flog me. Beat my ass with your whip. Make me get down and suck your rod. Make me lick your boots."

His suggestions were not lost on Butch, although he had already sketched out the scene in his mind.

As the sadistic thoughts swirled around in his mind, he began a more pronounced pumping. His cock was hard and throbbing, the jism rising at a rapid rate into the shaft of his cock, ready to exit from the cock's head.

"Thank you, Leatherman. Fuck me. Fuck my ass! It feels so good to have a real man's cock up my ass. I can feel your cock throbbing inside me." His head arched even further backward, his back muscles straining, his ass muscles clenching the manrod inside.

Butch began a frenzied fucking, gliding his cock out and then ramming it in. Harder and harder, faster and faster. With a mighty explosion, his cock erupted, his manjuices lubricating the cop's ass.

The two stood for some time as if frozen. It felt so good.

Butch finally removed his cock, leaving it to drip cum as he began to flog the cop's ass. Lash after lash. Leather strips cutting into the cop's asscheeks.

The cop started moaning again. "Fuck me with that whip. It feels so fucking good. Beat me. Beat my ass raw." Although Butch couldn't quite see his handiwork in the dark, he was certainly assured that the boy was enjoying it.

"Sir, I'm going to cum. Let me cum, please. My cock is so full of jism..." the boy pleaded.

"You'll wait until I tell you to cum, boy." With that, he gave the boy another series of hard lashes.

"Please, Sir," the boy said through gritted teeth, "I can't hold it...in... much longer."

"All right, boy, fuck that tree with your cum."

The boy only had to rub his cock against the tree once or twice before he let out a roar and cumjuice sprayed onto the trunk of the tree.

Once he had ejaculated, the boy stood silently. Butch untied him and forced him down on his knees. The boy was ordered to lick the drying cum off of his Master's cock. He was then pushed down to the ground where he began licking Butch's construction boots. And fuck, they were a challenge to any boy. Covered with mud and dirt from the landscaping projects Butch had worked on in the last week. The boy did a credible job, although it was hard to assess if he had gotten every spot in the darkness. The moon had disappeared behind a bank of clouds.

Once satisfied. Butch pulled him up and thrust his tongue in the boy's mouth. They kissed.

Butch escorted him into the house. Butch did have a puppy cage, but instead escorted Michael to the bedroom. The two men slept together with their arms wrapped around one another.

As he drifted off to sleep, Butch wondered what the future held for the two. "Maybe he's the one?"

Butch slept like a rock. The sun streamed through the window of the bedroom as Butch woke. He recalled last night's activities and turned to look at the playful pup. Unfortunately, the playful pup was not there. "Oh, shit," Butch thought, "another one night stand." About that time, Michael appeared, naked and handsome, with two steaming cups of coffee on a tray with a pitcher of milk and a sugar bowl.

"Good Morning, Sir, I hope you slept well." Michael said, with a smile on his face.

Butch nodded his thanks, returning the smile.

The two spent a leisurely morning in bed. Easy conversation. A little sexual play. Maybe Butch had found a boy all on his own.

All too soon, Michael had to return home and ready himself for work. But the two promised to see each other the next day.

Butch spent the rest of the day getting ready for the evening. This meant filling his tap and holding it in for the piss party.

And so had the rest of the men. Many of them came to the Club early. Drinking and driving, especially a motorcycle, was dangerous. The guys were encouraged to come to the Club, bring at least one six pack, and enjoy the company of the other Club members. Although they didn't want to spoil their images as rough and tough, the men participated in a 'covered dish' meal. Everybody brought something. This was a secret not to be shared by anyone outside the Club. Activities of the Club: Riding, smoking, drinking, fucking, flogging, whipping, pissing. Preparing a tuna noodle casserole was definitely not on the list.

There was a buzz of excitement and an increased level of testosterone within the Club walls. For the veterans, the pissing party was one of the highlights. The bathroom in the Club was padlocked. The rubber sheeting in the dark recesses of the Club had been laid out days before in anticipation of the event. The boys had been allowed to sleep longer than normal. It had been several days since any of them had been allowed to take a bath. The boy's bodies were grimy, exuding the natural smells of boysweat. Ripe pits and crotches. Drying cum and spittle. Most of the boys relished the feeling, only several were still not in the mindset of being submissive boys to a group of horny Leathermen.

The Leathermen stood around, leaning against the walls, rubbing their over-anxious cods and jocks. Consuming beer. Smoking cigars. All hot and all very horny for the events to begin.

Snake and Mick had proven capable DenMasters, readying the boys for the piss party. Kneeling, naked on the rubber sheeting. Hooded only until the festivities began. The boys were lined up, back to back in two rows. Hands behind their back, manacled back-to-back to another boy. Only the bootblack knelt by himself. He had gotten the most informal votes for the best boy.

The event was to begin a little later than 1800 hours, giving the guys ample opportunity to tank down as much beer as their bellies would hold. Max had drunk five. Phillippe- four.

The men's cocks were ready when Carson banged his fist on the table.

"Okay, men. Our favorite activity. The pissing party is about to begin. I want you to form a circle around our boys. Make each of them feel welcome! Drench them in piss. Aim for their mouths but don't forget your other favorite body parts on the boys! Piss like you mean it, fuckers!"

Snake and Mick removed the Leather hoods and the boys blinked as the overhead lights assaulted their eyes. Some of the boy's eyes widened as they viewed the over-anxious Leathermen with their sturdy cocks held erect with gloved hands.

The Club members were all rubbing their cocks, edging them to readiness and urgency. All cocks were fully erect. Throbbing with beer piss. Throbbing with bear piss. Throbbing with Leathermen's piss. Anxious to shower a boy. Most of them were thinking, "Shut the fuck up, Carson!"

Carson stopped talking, sensing the urgency. The anticipated pleasure. He too had a cockload of piss and wanted to shower the lawn boy with his own brand.

"Okay, Leathermen to your stations." The Leathermen jockeyed for position to stand in front of a favorite boy. Three fought for Joe, but Butch elbowed the other two out of the way. This boy was his.

Eventually the Leathermen formed a circle. Most boys would be drenched from the taps of two Leathered men.

Carson raised his hand with an imaginary gun. "Ready, aim, FIRE!"

And the pissing began. Max had chosen the cop and aimed a stream of golden piss which shot right into the boy's mouth. The boy gulped as the huge stream entered his throat. He kept gulping as the piss continued for some time. His chin was soon dribbling piss, it ran down on the boy's chest. Phillippe couldn't resist and pissed toward the hitchhiker, who momentarily had closed his mouth when the pissing began. It sprayed all over the boy's face before he finally opened his mouth. Phillippe alternated his considerable stream with the boy next to the hitchhiker, the slender young boy from the Leather store, who held his jaw open as far as he could.

Butch was taking great delight in shooting his stream into the hunky bootblack's mouth. The bootblack relished every drop, licking his lips, flicking his tongue out to catch more. Carson was happy because the golden boy, lawn boy, was taking his piss with a smile on his face. His eyes looked up at Carson as if he was climaxing. Carson looked down and the boy's cock was hard and throbbing. He momentarily diverted the flow to piss on the boy's cock. The cock arched upward. Rick and Mark, side by side, pissed into the young hustler's throat. Double the pleasure and the boy arched his body forward to catch both streams. No boy was forgotten as the men continued to piss.

As the streams began to ebb, the Leathermen marched up to the boys and soon the boys were licking the last drips of piss from the Leathermen's cocks. The Leathermen's cocks were soon filled again, but with another manjuice.

Pumping, thrusting, pulling a willing boy's head toward the shaft of the cock. Balls slamming against piss-drenched chins. Tongues licking piss off the cockhead.

Most of the men came within a few minutes in one massive fuckfest. There wasn't a boy's dry mouth in the house.

Once the Leathermen had been pleasured, they stood back to admire their work. The boy's bodies were sweaty, dirty, some with piss running down their chests. Lips being licked. Tongues darting in and out of the mouths of the willing boys.

Leathermen's cocks hanging limply, for the moment. Being caressed by gloved hands as the Leathermen headed for the refrigerator to replenish their taps.

The boys knelt silently while the Leathermen 'reloaded'. Most of the men lighted cigars and were alternating long guzzles of beer with long drags on their cigars.

The boys had knelt dutifully on the rubber sheeting. It had been the first chance most of the boys had had to review the Leathermen. Several were anxious to become a full-time sub. Jacob, the lawn boy, was really excited to be a part of this. He yearned for the approval of the Leathermen. He looked forward to the day when he would ride with them, in full black, ass-tight Leather. Joe was another willing boy. He wanted to please them all. Fuck, they were all so handsome in their big shit-kicking boots, pants with studded codpieces, cycle jackets with cockrings and chains on the epaulets. He wanted to serve them all- licking their boots and cocks, sucking on their man nipples, taking their piss, taking their cum. His cock was hardened by the thought of serving all twelve in one night. Even the most resistant had begun to realize the pleasure of serving a powerful man, anticipating the day when you would be walking proudly with a man down the street. The black Leathers gleaming and shining in the sunlight or underneath a streetlamp. In particular, the cop, who had resisted strenuously, now wanted to be part of the brotherhood. Tough, rough, real men- not a fucking cop that would sit in a patrol car, issuing tickets to people who were going five miles over the posted speed limit. He wanted to ride- with his legs straddling a cycle. His cock outlined in a codpiece and pressed against the asscheeks of a proud Leatherman cyclist. His man, who he would serve. Defying convention. Giving the finger to the world- most of whom sat at home and watched reruns of a cop show. He envisioned himself in a full Leather cop uniform, tall black boots. Someone he would have a boy go down on his boots. "Lick them, boy. Worship my boots," he would say. Slap the boy roughly when the boy stopped for a second. Unrelenting on the boy's punishment until the boots were spit-shined. Fuck, yeah, he thought, as his cock hardened.

It did not go unnoticed by Max who had been watching the boys out of the corner of his eye.

He sauntered over to the cop.

"Looks like you got a boner, there, boy."

"Yes, Sir. Proud of it, Sir," the cop replied.

Max reached the toe of his heavy boot upward, connecting with the hardened cock.

The boy relished the feeling. "Thank you, Sir."

"Can you lean forward, boy?" The cop was manacled back-to-back to the first hustler captured. He did lean forward as far as he could. The head of his cock just touched the rubber sheeting.

Max stepped on the cock with his boot. The boy momentarily flinched, but said, "That feels so good, Sir. I wish you would do that to my cock every night, Sir."

Max massaged the shaft of the cock with the sole of the boot. The boy's cock lengthened. Max slid the boot back and forth. The boy's cock was now throbbing, veins prominently appearing along the shaft.

"Sir," the boy moaned, "please let me cum."

Max withdrew his boot, "Sorry, boy, you can't do that yet. Against the Club rules." He leaned down into the boy's face and said, "I'm taking you home, boy. You're gonna be my boy. I'm gonna fuck you until you're raw, boy."

The boy was breathing heavily, his cock reacting to Max's promise. "Sir, I would truly enjoy that. You are a handsome Leatherman and I would be proud to be your boy."

Max chuckled, "Yes, you would, boy. Yes, you would."

Max withdrew as the boy's cock spurted a few drops of precum. The boy couldn't keep his eyes off Max after that. "He's my Leatherman and I'm his boy."

Carson announced the second session of manpissing. And the Leathermen hastily formed a circle. Every man was on his honor to choose a different subject although several were set on pissing on the same candidate. Max, in particular.

He was a reasonable man, however, and relinquished his position to Rick. They had been buddies for a long time. "After all, that boy is gonna be in my dungeon every night once the initiation rites are concluded," Max thought.

Rick liked to give the boy a golden shower from head to crotch, using his apparatus like a fire hose. He enjoyed seeing the golden dew drip down a boy's forehead and a boy's tongue reaching for each drop as it dropped off the boy's nose or cheeks. Snake, on the other hand, made his submissive lean his head back as far as he could. Snake delivered a stream right down the handsome hustler's throat. He had taken a special interest in the first one retrieved from the alley. He was feisty. He had wrestled longer in his bondage equipment than anyone else. It was kind of like taming a bucking bronco. Snake enjoyed a challenge like this. As he continued a long, satisfying piss, he thought, "I'll tie you up, boy, leave you in place for a weekend. You'll be hungry for mancock, manpiss, and mancum, by the time I come and retrieve your sorry ass."

The third night was drawing to an end as the boys ingested the last few drops from the pissladen manrods. The boys had done well. After announcing that the fourth and final night of the initiation rites would be assplay night, Carson appointed John and Chuck as DenMasters for the night. The Leathermen were satisfied for the most part as they placed their cocks in their cods and headed out on their cycles.

BRUTALITY

Without his partner, Carson decided to take a spin on his cycle. It was a beautiful night and there was nothing better than feeling the wind rushing against your Leathers. Your Leathered legs hugging your Harley. Looking tough and masculine and feeling every bit of that- fucking the world. Carson decided to travel to their former rendezvous and beat off in the thicket of woods where they had tied up the hitchhiker. It was a solitary area and Carson enjoyed the primitive nature of it.

He reached his destination and dismounted his bike. He followed the trail into the woods and located a sturdy tree to lean against. He pulled out his cigar case and lighted a big fucker. He relaxed, smoking his cigar, lazily stroking his cod. There was a cool breeze blowing and Carson was glad he had on full Leather.

Traffic zoomed past with frightening speed and frightening regularity. "Damn," he thought, "there's a lot of traffic out." He heard a number of cycles go by, enjoying the good evening air just like him.

He returned to stroking and smoking. Losing himself in the reverie of his cockplay. Thinking of the boys in his dungeon. Thinking of that cute little blonde boy raking leaves- damn he would make a good houseboy. Thinking of fucking John.

By and by, he realized that there was the unmistakable sound of three or four cycles idling. The unmistakable sound of leaves crunching and branches snapping. Heavy booted feet. Carson hastened to put his cock back in his pants. He tried to assess where the other bikers were. He didn't want any trouble- never had it before, but then again, he had usually ridden with other members of the Club.

As he attempted to exit quietly, he tripped over a branch and fell facedown into a pile of brush. A booted foot was standing on top of it.

"Well, hell, what do we have here?" said the biker. A big burly guy with a chest-length beard.

As Carson attempted to pick himself up, the biker pulled him up with one hand.

"I'm Carson..." as Carson reached out his hand. It was squeezed by a big meaty hand. "They call me 'Fuckem', because that's what I usually say to any situation, just 'Fuckem'".

The men laughed. His associates were just as big as he was. Big, meaty men. Fucking hot Leather skins covering their massive bodies. Big shit-kicking engineer boots.

"So, what are you guys doing tonight?" Carson asked.

"Looking for trouble," he answered.

Carson's panic button went up a notch. He was one man surrounded by four big, strapping men. He could try to make a run for it. Wouldn't make it. Carson was a substantial man and wasn't easily bullied or frightened, but these guys could beat the shit out of him.

"What kind of trouble?" Carson asked, attempting to remain calm.

"Oh, a little drinkin', a lot of whorin'," the burly man responded.

"Oh, shit, and I know who the whore is gonna be," thought Carson.

"Tell, you what, guys, let me lead you to the Wayward Inn- lots of guys there- take your pick..." said Carson as he attempted to move forward.

'Fuckem' caught him around the neck and replied, "No, I think we found the whore we want..." and he laughed sadistically.

Two of the associates wrapped their arms around Carson. He struggled vigorously but these guys were a lot bigger than he was.

They escorted him to the tree that he had been standing against and quickly tied him with bondage rope. He was roped facing the tree.

His pants were yanked down as 'Fuckem' rubbed his massive shaft. Despite his fear, Carson had taken cock up his ass before. He and John played with dildos. What he was fearful of was that this was not play, this was impending rape. 'Fuckem' slid his cock up Carson's hole. The burly guy was surprised when Carson didn't moan. He just stood silently. Actually, the big man's cock felt pretty good.

Carson said, "Fuck, yeah, that feels good, big man. Now, get it hard. Pump it."

The big burly man was agitated at the comments and slapped Carson across the face, "Shut the fuck up. I am hard."

Carson knew he was pushing it, but he said, "That's all you got and you call yourself a Leatherman. Ram it in me. Fuck me hard. I like it."

The man was becoming more annoyed by Carson's comments. He pulled a black bandana from his back pocket and shoved it in Carson's mouth.

Carson arched his ass outward, expanding and contracting the asscheeks, attempting to pull the cock in. 'Fuckem ' was at maximum length and his cock wouldn't go any further.

Carson had worked the bandana out of his mouth and spitting it out, taunted the biker once more. "That's it? Come on, someone else step up to the plate. Fuck my ass- I want a real assfucking. Tell 'Little Dick' to come back when he's grown up."

The big burly guy slapped Carson a few more times, ramming his cock hard into Carson's hole. Despite the pain Carson felt, he would never show it. After all, Carson was a sadist. He could dole it out, but he could also take it.

One of the men pushed 'Fuckem' aside. He had pulled out his meat and was rubbing it with his big calloused hands. "Let me have a go at Mr. SmartMouth."

He rammed his cock into Carson's throbbing hole, clenching Carson's asscheeks.

Carson began again, "Fuck, stop putting your finger in my hole. Use your dick. Oh, wait, is that your cock? Tell, 'Fuckem' to try again. Better than your pencil dick…" Carson got slapped repeatedly by the second guy.

The two others rammed their cocks up Carson's hole, but he did not relent. While their cocks were tearing at his insides, he continued the smart-assed comments. The guys were getting more frustrated.

"Hell, it ain't no fun, if they don't squeal like pigs," one of them said.

"Guess this guy has been around the block a few too many times… his hole is stretched too much to give us pleasure."

"Wait," said Fuckem, "I got an idea." He pushed his buddy aside and inserted the gloved fingers of his meaty fist.

Now, that hurt. Carson restrained himself from outwardly wincing, but the big fucker's fist hurt. Calming his inner thoughts, he remarked, "Hell, I've produced bigger shits. But thank you for it because I think your fist is gonna loosen my inner workings. Keep going, buddy. You'll get a load you didn't expect."

"Holy fuck," one of the guys remarked, "I'm not into scat." He marched back toward his cycle. The other men followed suit.

'Fuckem' was the last to leave, but not before kicking Carson in the ass with his steel-toed boot. That fucking hurt as well. They left Carson tied to the tree with his pants around his knees. His ass throbbed like hell. The cockplay was mild, but the guy's fist had really hurt his rectum.

He waited for the cycles to crank and as he heard them speed away, he began the task of loosening his ropes. These men knew what they were doing- it took him a good forty-five minutes to extricate himself from the roping. He massaged his wrists, pulled up his pants, and exited the woods. As he approached his cycle, he noticed that the men had flattened his tires. "Bastards," he thought as he began walking the long walk back to the Club. At least they hadn't used the knife, or whatever they had punctured the tires with, on him.

Cars whizzed past but no one stopped- very few people would stop and pick up a man in full Leathers. Carson's ass ached. Probably more because he was pissed about his bike's tires. He thought of every dirty word and applied it to the bikers. By the time, he had walked two or three miles, he had calmed down considerably. In fact, his ass felt good now. Every Leatherman needs his hole stretched sooner or later.

As he continued to walk, Carson heard the thundering of Harleys approaching.

"Fuck," he thought, as he ducked into a ditch. It might be the same bikers looking for him again. As the cycles passed him, it was Snake, Rick, and two other bikers- probably other members of the Club.

He crawled out of the ditch and yelled for them to stop, but not before they had already sped past.

"Shit," he yelled. He continued walking.

It was 0630 hours and Carson was still walking toward the Club. Fortunately, a farmer on his way to a farmer's market stopped and gave Carson a lift. The Club never looked so inviting! He staggered in.

ASSPLAY

As Carson entered the Club, John rushed over to him.

"What the fuck happened to you?" as he supported his partner, easing him down into a chair.

Carson quickly recounted the brutality at the hands of the bikers.

John was ready to mount up and catch the fuckers by himself, but Carson talked him down from his anger.

John loaded Carson on the back of his cycle and took him home. After giving Carson a hot shower, he placed him in their bed and then went off to take care of the two submissives who had been in bondage since the night before. John fed his partner as well as the two boys. The day evaporated quickly. John called Snake to help him retrieve Carson's cycle. It was handy having Snake as a Club member and personal friend. John also called on Mark, asking him to fill in for him as DenMaster. Readying the boys for the final night.

It was soon time to return to the Club for the last night of the initiation. Carson insisted he was fine despite the blisters on his feet. His ass was sore too, but he enjoyed that sensation and went about dressing in his heavy black Leathers.

This night was designated for Assplay and no Leatherman would want to miss it. Every Club member came armed with dildos, rubber gloves, rockhard cocks, and lots of lube.

Chuck and Mark readied the boys for the final 'assault'. The boys were once again manacled to Posts No. #1-7. All were facing the posts of course.

Max was the first Club member to arrive. He wore his crotch-high Wescos and a studded metallic cod, which jutted forward with his big mandick hard and horny. He viewed the asses, rubbing the already swollen head of his cock encased in the Leather cod.

Chuck and Mark filled him in on what had transpired. "I say we mount up and find those fuckers..." Chuck and Mark attempted to calm him down, but he didn't want to be calmed down. He was ready to mix it up. Assfuck the fuckers.

"Carson's okay," Chuck assured him, "A few blisters on his feet from walking so far."

"The fuckers damaged his cycle..." Max said. He wouldn't be placated.

More Club members began to arrive and they were of a similar opinion to Max.

Snake arrived with the bad news that Carson's cycle was damaged, apparently the vindictive fuckers had poured water in the tank, clogging up the fuel lines and doing considerable damage to the cycle's internal workings.

The Club members were riled up. They wanted to head out as a pack and confront the assholes who had inflicted the damage. Carson and John arrived just as Snake was filling the guys in. Carson was pissed. He counted the members- only Butch was missing. He hastily called a meeting of the Club.

Before Carson had a chance to speak, Max roared, "Let's ride and get the fuckers. Any asswipe that damages another's guy cycle deserves punishment." The Club members agreed. Carson was ready for revenge, surrounded by his loyal buddies. It was a consensus of the Club members that they would go out on patrol and find the bikers that did the damage to Carson's cycle and ass. The final night of the boy's initiation rites was suspended for the evening. Carson and John stayed behind to take care of the boys. The nine men left the Club and mounted up. They roared off into the night. From a description of the leader, Snake had a pretty good idea who the guys might be and where they might be congregating. The Wayward Inn. Before they left, however, the guys agreed they would not engage the dirty bikers inside the Club. They agreed that they would take the confrontation outside.

The cycles thundered down the paved highway, gleaming in the moonlight.

The Leathermen's cocks were pulsing inside their Leather cods. Leather gloves holding tightly onto the handlebars. Leathered legs hugging the sides of the cycle. Fucking revenge in their hearts.

The Leathermen arrived at the Wayward Inn, spitting gravel as they parked. There were cycles parked outside, but there were always cycles parked outside.

The Leathermen walked menacingly in. Heads turned as the nine substantial men swept through the Club. Rick approached the bartender and described the leader. "No," the bartender replied, "they were here. Raising hell. Antagonizing the customers. Loud, obnoxious. I felt helpless- I don't have any back-up tonight."

"You do now, Buddy. We'll act as sentries. Hope they return. We've got a surprise for them."

"Well," the bartender replied, "I hope they don't return. I don't want trouble."

Rick assured him that his Club members would not cause any trouble in the bar.

The bartender seemed to relax and offered the Club members beer on the house.

The Club members conferred and agreed that three of them would stay while the others cruised the nearby roads. They broke up into teams of three.

Max, along with Snake and Phillippe, led his contingent back to their cycles and they were soon cruising the roadways.

About twenty minutes out, Max spotted the gleam of chrome on the side of the road. Four cycles were parked in a wooded area. Max rode about two hundred feet further down the road and motioned for the guys to pull off on the shoulder. He conferred with his Leather soldiers before they began walking back to the area where he had seen the cycles. He heard loud voices, laughing, cursing.

The Leathermen approached stealthily.

Four bikers were lounging against trees, smoking. Six-packs of emptied beer bottles were scattered at their feet. Their voices were slurred- they were pissing drunk.

Snake looked at the faces as best he could. He just couldn't tell if it was the guy known as 'Fuckem'. He was pretty well-known as a mean fucker in biker circles. Had been in 'Nam, which apparently had really screwed him up. Had been incarcerated for brutalizing a number of his own platoon. One or two of the guys had been sodomized so severely that they had been messed up for months.

"I think that's 'Fuckem'," whispered Snake, "I just can't be sure. May as well get this over with."

The Leathermen advanced confidently.

"Heard you wanted to mix it up, 'Fuckem'?" Snake said in a loud voice.

The bearded man's head snapped around. "What the fuck?" he said.

"We're here to ask you a few questions, asswipe," Snake said.

'Fuckem' bellied up to Snake, sticking his face right into Snake's.

"Yeah, bitch, what do you want to ask me?"

"You played with one of our Club members last night. You messed up his cycle."

"So, what the fuck if we did?"

"We're here to even the score."

By this time, 'Fuckem's buddies were standing even with 'Fuckem' trying to stare down the other men. The Leathermen of G.O.L.D. weren't so easily intimidated. Three against four.

One of 'Fuckem's men took the first gut punch at Max. Max easily deflected the meaty fist and twisted it behind the biker. What Max didn't anticipate was an engineer boot to the groin. Max winced in pain, but didn't let his grip loosen. Hard fists were swung. Booted feet kicked and stomped. These were hard men, who fought to win. Fortunately, the Club members were layered in heavy Leather and the Leather took some of the abuse. It also restricted some of their movements. 'Fuckem's buddies all carried knives and the knives were soon drawn. Fortunately, all the guys who rode that night for the Club had worn heavy gauntlets and were able to deflect the knife thrusts.

The Club men were ramping up their anger as Max head-butted one of the opposing bikers. He went down. Max placed a heavily-booted foot on the man's throat.

"You ain't going nowhere, fucker," as Max reached down and gutpunched him four or five times. The man lay heaving on the ground.

While Max was leaning over the man, another attacked him from behind, but Snake, anticipating the action, encircled the attacker's neck and held him in a tight grip. The guy began choking, clawing at Snake's vise-like arm. Snake turned the man around and kneed him sharply in the groin. The guy doubled over and Snake kicked him in the ass until the man fell on the ground.

'Fuckem' attacked Phillippe, little realizing the man was tightly packed with muscle. 'Fuckem' was strong and the men wrestled for some time.

He got Phillippe in a choke-hold and held a knife to Phillippe's neck.

"Try any more shit and I'll cut your pal's throat," he hissed. The first drops of blood appeared on Phillippe's neck.

The Club members stopped in mid-action. Holding their hands up. 'Fuckem' walked toward a tree with the knife still tightly held against Phillippe's neck.

"Charlie, get the rope. We're gonna have a hogtying party. And you know I like to buttfuck hogs." The four bikers laughed as Charlie went to retrieve the rope from his cycle.

Max and Snake looked at each other. As if on a football field, they communicated a silent plan of action. It would have to be swift or else Phillipe's throat would be sliced.

"'Fuckem', why don't you take me instead?" Snake said.

"Nah, I like this pretty boy better." 'Fuckem' answered.

"My hole's tighter. Phillippe's a whore."

"Then I'll have both of you." 'Fuckem' flatly stated.

HERE I COME
TO SAVE THE DAY...

Butch couldn't keep his hands off of Michael's ass. There was something so erotic about seeing a cop's ass in tight cotton twill fabric. Especially when you had seen the same sexy ass naked, tied to a tree. As promised, the two were rendezvousing the next day, in the afternoon. Michael had been on duty for third shift, but was now on his own time. He had stopped by Butch's house and the two were quickly locked in a tight embrace. It was another incredibly beautiful day and the two decided to go for a cycle ride.

"Leave your cop uniform on." Butch ordered, "I want to molest you while you're still wearing it." His cock was hardening as he viewed the handsome man in his uniform, spitshined boots to the knee, tight Damascus gloves covering his hands. His Sam Brown belt creating a furrow between his muscular pecs.

"Yes, Sir, your orders are to be obeyed, Sir."

Michael crawled on behind Butch, his crotch area tightly pressed into Butch's ass.

The two rode for some time, Michael's cock lengthening in his pants, pressed tightly against Butch's ass. Butch was fully aroused and simply wanted to find a secluded place where the two could fuck.

Every place he looked there were cars or people, or both, out enjoying the mild weather and cloudless skies.

Butch suddenly remembered the story of the hitchhiker's capture told to him by Phillippe and the secluded woods where the unwilling boy had been tied to a tree. Butch always carried his basic S&M supplies in his saddlebags. 'Be Prepared' was his motto. He had lifted the phrase from the Boy Scouts which he had belonged to as a kid. He turned to the left and was headed to the area. He had been riding for about twenty minutes with Michael's cock knocking on his backdoor when he spotted cycles off to the side of the road. "Damn," Butch thought, "that looks like Snake's cycle." A closer look revealed the distinct emblem of a snake on the tank. "Those fuckers, they're probably out there buggering somebody else." He also recognized the cycles of Max and Phillippe. As he gazed in the direction of a distinct dirt path, he noted four more cycles. An unknown cycleman was retrieving something from his saddlebag. It looked like a coil of coarse hemp rope. The guy apparently did not see them and disappeared down the dirt path into the woods.

"Shit," Butch said, "I wonder if those are the bikers that fucked Carson?"

"Let's go investigate," Michael said, as he checked his holster. His gun was still intact, of course. Although at the moment, he was an off duty cop.

"Let's take it slowly, Buddy," Butch warned, "from what I heard these guys are mean fuckers."

They proceeded cautiously, Michael leading the way. After all, he had more experience in these matters.

They ducked in bushes and inched their way carefully to the dirt path. The unmistakable sound of laughter and taunting could be heard.

Michael was hunched low, stealthily advancing toward the origin of the sounds. Butch followed closely behind.

As they neared the approach, two of the bikers were tying someone to a tree with the coarse hemp.

"It looks like Phillippe," Butch whispered. He could see Max being held tightly by another man. It looked as if a knife was being held to Max's throat. The third guy was holding someone, he couldn't tell who- it must be Snake.

"Shit, they've got them at knifepoint." as he saw the guys nearest Phillippe brandishing knives near Phillippe's nips.

"I think I may slice your tits off, boy," 'Fuckem' announced as he pressed his body against Phillippe's. Phillippe remained calm, although he was heaving inwardly.

The other guy, Charlie, was behind Phillippe tightening the ropes around Phillippe's chest and arms.

"Save one for me, I want to see this fucker bleed."

Michael drew his gun as he advanced closer and closer to the two men surrounding Phillippe.

They were engrossed in what they were doing and were momentarily unaware that they were being stalked.

Michael took careful aim and fired once, wounding Charlie in the shoulder. Charlie let loose of the ropes and grabbed his shoulder which had been grazed.

"What the fuu...?" 'Fuckem' started as he took a round in his shoulder. He dropped the knife and grabbed his left shoulder.

This gave Max and Snake the opportunity of surprise and they wrestled the two remaining bikers to the ground.

Max stepped on the man's wrist who was still holding tight to his knife. Max jumped on the man's wrist with his booted foot, hearing a distinct crunch as the man's wrist was broken. Snake executed the same maneuver.

Butch and Michael rushed in. Butch quickly untied Phillippe while Michael held the gun on 'Fuckem'. Charlie was cowering, still holding his own bleeding shoulder.

The score was now five to four. The rough hemp ropes were quickly tied around the four bikers' wrists and ankles, cut into suitable lengths with their own knives.

The four Club members and Michael convened and argued what should be done with the four bikers.

Max wanted to fuck them all.

A plan was formulated. The four bikers were relieved of their keys and their cycles were soon in the woods next to their trussed bodies. As Michael relieved them of their keys, he found packets of what looked like cocaine. He looked in the saddlebags of the cycles, discovering even more coke.

"Just what I needed..." Michael said. Fortunately, he had remained in his uniform which included his dispatch unit.

He called into headquarters and explained that he had been ambushed by four drug dealers after he had finished his shift. He told his superior officer that they had dragged him into a wooded area and were going to mess him up, threatening to execute him. He had managed to wound two in self-defense. Michael made up the next part of the story- four bikers out for a ride had noticed the struggle and had come to his rescue. With their help, they had tied up the scum. "Send back-up units," Michael calmly stated, as he gave his superior the location. "I'm going to escort the men who rescued me to the hospital- they all have knife wounds from the struggle that ensued." His superior wanted him to stay at the scene, but Michael calmly said, "One of the heroes is bleeding pretty badly- losing blood rapidly. Better go, Chief." Before the Chief had a chance to respond, he and the four Club members exited the scene.

The four Club members and Michael returned to Butch's house where they dressed the knife wounds. Fortunately, they were only flesh wounds.

Max was furious, fuming, "I only needed twenty minutes to shove my cock up all their asses and give them a lasting impression of 'Mad' Max."

"You can visit them in prison," Michael said.

Max grinned, "Hey, I have connections at the prison…"

Leaving that thought firmly planted in his mind, the five rode back to the Wayward Inn. They kicked back a couple of beers and then retrieving the others who had stood guard. They rode back to the Club, having reclaimed their turf from 'Fuckem' and the other bikers.

The Club was quiet as Carson and John placed the seven submissives back in what had become their sleeping chamber.

Carson and John were anxious to hear what had transpired. The guys stormed in from the Wayward Inn.

They soon recounted what had happened.

"You can come with me to the prison when I visit our newly-found fuckholes," Max promised.

Carson was grateful for the news. He was still upset about his cycle and it would take an activity just like that to avenge the wrongs.

ASSPLAY REVISITED

The Club members reconvened the next evening. Once again, the boys had been trussed into place with them facing their respective posts.

It had been a long initiation, but the boys had done well. Not one was lagging in spirit. They were placed against their posts, naked, except for their boots. Jim and Mick had volunteered to serve as DenMasters for the night.

Carson called a brief meeting for the Club members. He recounted what had transpired in the last twenty-four hours and expressed his deep gratitude for the support of his brotherhood. "I'm not upset about the assfucking- it felt pretty damned good. But I am upset about my cycle. You guys have proven to me that we are Leather brothers and you will do anything for a Club member. And I thank you for it."

"Hey," Max bellowed, "I'm planning a picnic to the prison. I have some fucking cherries I want to pop." Everyone laughed.

When Carson asked if there were any considerations, Butch raised his hand.

"I'd like to propose that Michael be made an honorary Club member for service to the Club beyond any reasonable call of duty. He endangered his own life for the life of the Club members."

There was little discussion before Michael was nominated to be a full member. The first submissive to be made a full-member.

"I'll be glad to tell him of the honor," Butch volunteered, "I have my own way of showing my gratitude." Once again the guys laughed.

"Okay, men, I see that you've brought your toys. For the last time, we'll draw numbers to see who gets to plug the boys' asses first."

Every cock in the place was bulging inside its Leather enclosure. Ready for action. Ready to drip, throb, thrust, and cum, shooting up a willing sub's ass.

Mark was the first to choose and he selected the hot ass of the bootblack. He positioned himself behind the willing ass of the even more willing boy.

His cock was throbbing as he rubbed his codpiece against the boy's beautiful ass. The asscheeks were spread as far as the boy could get them in his trussed position. Mark began a slow, rhythmic massage with his cod to get the asscheeks spread even further. He massaged his cock with one hand and slowly slapped the boy's asscheeks. The boy's head arched backward. A moan escaped his plugged mouth.

Mark slowly unsnapped his cod, releasing his meaty cock and pendulous balls. He rubbed a little lube on the head and more lube on the boy's mineshaft. He slowly worked his cock up the boy's hole. The cock arched further, hard and firm, throbbing with intensity as Mark placed his gloved hands on the boy's asscheeks. He began pumping with a steadier rhythm. The boy moaned, his head arching backward and forward. The boy was breathing heavily, his muscular arms straining against the chains which bound his hands to the post.

Mark began breathing heavily as his cock took the boy's ass as his own. Mark pressed his Leathered chest against the boy's back. His hips pumped in and out, in and out. His cock was throbbing. Thrusting. Exploring. The man's cum was rising in the shaft of his cock as he began a more frenzied pumping. He could feel the cum rising closer and closer to its point of exit.

He clenched the boy's asscheeks with gloved hands as he pressed his Leathered body until the two bodies melded into one fuck machine.

The boy's cock was hard and throbbing, a glistening of precum was evident in the piss slit.

Mark began pounding his cock into the hole. He reached around and grabbed the boy's cock and began a frenzied pumping as if it was his own.

The boy moaned. Mark's head arched backward, his Leathered body slamming against the boy's naked, handsome body.

He pulled his cock out. It was dripping, but had not shot a load of jism.

He continued the vigorous massaging of the boy's cock. "Don't you cum, boy," Mark warned the bootblack, "not until I say so." The boy gritted his teeth against the plug in his mouth. This was going to be difficult because he was fully aroused.

Mark stepped away momentarily and extracted a cigar from his jacket pocket. He clipped the end and lighted the cigar.

Mark blew several smoke rings toward the ceiling. The boy was twisting in his restraints. He wanted to play with his dick.

Mark's cock was beginning to settle down. He flicked it occasionally just to keep it from becoming totally flaccid. He removed his jacket and shirt.

The boy continued to moan and twist in his restraints. His dick was still throbbing, bobbing up and down, seeking a gloved hand.

Mark stepped back into position and went through the procedure for the second time. The boy's cock was still glistening with precum, but he had not shot. He was a good boy.

Mark eased his cock back into place in the boy's hole. He began another massage of the boy's asscheeks. The boy was wild, once again gritting his teeth against the Leather plug in his mouth.

Mark pressed his naked torso against the boy's back, rubbing his man nips against the boy's back. The boy was even more aroused as Mark reached around and began rolling the boy's nips between his gloved fingers.

The boy was in agony. His dick was throbbing, pulsing, ready to cum.

Mark pulled his cock out once more, hard and glistening with precum in the slit. He kept it hard and firm, rubbing it with the long, black cigar.

The boy was twisting, moaning, pulling against his restraints.

Mark reached the lighted cigar toward the boy's left nip. The sting was so fucking erotic. The boy's cock pulsed up and down, the veins on the shaft fulling engorged with blood, precum waiting to be released. The boy gritted his teeth, now biting into the Leather plug.

Mark circled the right tit with the lighted end of the cigar. The boy mumbled something, in a pleading manner, but Mark ignored it.

He reinserted the cigar in his mouth, spit on his manpole, and began rolling and squeezing the boy's nips with his gloved hands.

He slowly reinserted his manrod into the boy's shaft. He began a frenzied pumping and within minutes, shot a load of jism up the boy's receptive hole.

He left it in place for a long time.

After what seemed an eternity, he gave the boy permission to shoot. With Mark's gloved hands rubbing it, the boy needed no further coaxing as he shot a load which landed on the post and splattered on the floor.

"Good boy," Mark said, as he slapped the boy's asscheeks, "Good boy."

All the Leathermen on 'Post' duty wanted to prolong the assfucking session as long as possible. Most had developed scenes similar to Mark's session. After the days of captivity, the boys were uniformly receptive to the Leathermen's desires and needs. Not one of them had faltered. After cumming, the Club members of the first round had reluctantly relinquished their 'Posts' to the remaining guys who had patiently waited for the second round. There wasn't a dry cock in the house that night.

After such a rigorous day, many of the Leathermen wanted to get some rest and so, Initiation #4 ended earlier than the other sessions. Carson, as President, declared it a great success. He and John would be staying the night, cleaning the boys up and readying them for the next night of Declaration of Intent. For the first time, the boys would be allowed to shower and remove the layers of dirt, cum, sweat, and piss. They had all performed beautifully and would be inducted into the Club as Sub Boys.

Some of the Club members offered to stay and help and so, Carson went home to take care of his submissives. The two boys at home were not needed for the Club. He and John were secretly grateful.

DECLARATION OF INTENT

Each boy was to be assigned to a Sir. The Sir was responsible for the boy's further training as a submissive, taking the boy into his home and educating him into proper service as a Leatherboy of the Club. All the boys had passed the initiation rites, but now the real training began.

The night of assignment was a festive event and the guys arrived slowly, their boots shined, their handsome Leathers outlining their masculine bodies, their horny cocks bulging. The men would participate in a lottery, much like the drawing for the four nights of initiation, for each of the available boys. Even a man with a submissive was eligible. Carson and John felt slightly guilty, for they had the potential of having four subs at one time. They did not feel the need to tell the Club members about the two boys that were tied up in their basement.

Butch arrived with his handsome boy Michael in tow. Michael was once again in the Leather cop uniform. Butch kept him close at hand. In fact, he had collared Michael with a studded dog collar and held a leash in his gloved hand. Michael would not stray far or the puppy would have to be whipped.

Of the twelve Club members, five already had subs who had elected to stay with their Sirs long after the training session was over. Max, Mick, Jim, Phillippe, and Mark brought their boys with them. The boys, over the past year, had earned their Leathers and for the evening, were attired in vests, jocks, chaps, and boots. For the moment, the five boys were sent to a private room while Club business was transacted. Michael remained.

When all twelve had arrived, Carson called the meeting to order.

"Men, it is a proud day in the history of our Club. This year's harvesting has yielded a fine crop of boys, all of whom have survived the initiation rites and proven themselves worthy of our Club. As you know, we harvested seven. There are obviously twelve Masters among us and one handsome submissive. I want to officially welcome Michael into the Club." Applause and hooting interrupted Carson's speech. When the applause had died down, Carson continued, "Thank you, Michael, for your service to the Club. We will reward you not only with our gift to a new boy in the Club, a Leather jockstrap, but also with a colors vest." With that Rick opened the supply closet and presented Michael with a vest, proudly displaying the Club's name on the back. "We realize that your job requires discretion, but hope that you will wear it to Club functions and when you are out cycling."

"Yes, Sir, thank you, Sir," Michael responded, "I will wear it with the utmost respect, Sir."

Michael was greeted as the newest member of the Club with slaps on the back and friendly groping of his private parts. His ass filled out the Leather pants nicely and his muscular chest pressed against the Leather shirt. He placed the jockstrap over his pants, causing the guys to break out in applause.

Michael put the Leather vest on and then went and knelt behind Butch.

"Now, we have an important task ahead of us. We must question the boys of their intent to serve as submissive boys within the Club. Jim, will you bring out Candidate #1." Jim was the Parliamentarian of the Club.

The hustler, last seen in an alley one week before, was led out. He was naked except for his boots. He was not hooded, however. He was ordered to kneel before the Club members.

"Candidate #1, you were brought here a week ago to endure the initiation rites of the Gods of Leather Discipline. You have proven yourself worthy of the Club and have proven yourself worthy of being called a Leatherboy. Is it now your intention to declare before this meeting of Leathermen that you accept these responsibilities seriously and without reservation and that you will always uphold the standards of the Club, never defaming it through thought, word or deed? If so, signify by saying 'I make this my Declaration of Intent to serve as a submissive in the Gods of Leather Discipline Club. "

The submissive repeated the phrase. The boy was made to prick his finger several times in order to sign his name in blood on the Declaration of Intent, transferring ownership of the boy to the Club.

"Congratulations, boy. You are now a part of the Club," Carson said, as he presented the boy with a Leather jockstrap. The boy was required to wear it when attending meetings at the Club.

"You will be trained by your new Sir," Carson declared, as he reached for a white slip of paper held in his Muir cap, "who is... Snake." Snake marched proudly forward. He had been eyeing the boy since the first night. He was rough around the edges, a street tough. Snake liked that it in a boy- feistiness, experienced. Snake was ready and placed a posture collar around the boy's neck. He led the boy back to where he was standing and ordered the boy to kneel.

Candidate #2, the other street hustler, was also quickly initiated. His new Sir was Rick.

Rick stepped up to the boy and hooked his arm around the boy's neck.

"Come on with me, boy," Rick said, "I want you to teach me all about alley sex."

The boy grinned.

Candidate #3 was the cop. His newly-assigned department had been told by a very convincing member of the Club that the Officer was disgusted with their seeming indifference to the poor treatment he had received, by giving him a worthless car, and he had headed back home. Their attitude was apparently 'Fuck him'. He was now happy with his new life and marched proudly out to the 'arena' where he knelt with his head held high. He willingly took the oath, signed the paper, and as fate would have it, his new Sir was Butch.

"Fuck, the lottery is rigged," complained Max, "he now has two sub cops for his own pleasure. What the fuck?"

"You can come over and play with my boy toys," Butch said as he grinned broadly.

"That's better, you fucker."

But Butch added, "Once I've played with them."

Candidate #4 was Tim, the young man from the Leather store. He had proven himself a very willing boy and anyone of the Daddies would have been glad to have him as their boy. Obedient, respectful, already into Leather, and a painpig. Mick's name was selected as the boy's Sir. Mick was beaming- he had not forgotten the fucking hot time the two had in the alley behind the Wayward Inn.

When Candidate #5, Joe the bootblack, was brought forward, there were hoots and yells, and loud applause. By popular vote, Joe was the favorite of the group. He had performed extremely well and every guy in the Club wanted him as their submissive. Hell, every boot you owned would be polished. And, oh yeah, there was also the cock servicing he would perform, and everyone remembered those pink nips hidden among the black fur of his body. After the oath had been administered, Joe stood calmly with his engineer boots spread wide apart. His handsome meat hung between his legs. His arms were placed behind his back.

"You will be trained by your new Sir," Carson announced, as he pulled the white slip of paper from his Muir cap, "who is… de Lorenzo." Simultaneously, the two let out war whoops. de Lorenzo rushed over, picked Joe up, and slung him over his broad shoulder. de Lorenzo was beaming and even though Joe was trying to suppress emotion, he too had a broad grin on his face. There was a mutual attraction between the two from the moment de Lorenzo sat in the bootblack's chair. Both could not wait for the evening to end, for pleasures awaited at the home of Joe's Sir.

Just two candidates remained. Candidate #6, the hitchhiker in cowboy boots, was brought out. He had initially resisted the Club's plan of action, but now embraced it as well. Chuck's name was chosen to be the hitchhiker's Sir. And finally, the last candidate was brought out. It was Jacob who had been tending his grandma's lawn when he was forced to submit to the Club members. Jacob was having the time of his life. His face beamed as he received his Leather jockstrap. He secretly hoped that he would be going home with Carson and John and as if fate stepped in, John's name was chosen.

"Come on, boy," John said. He added mysteriously, "There's always room for one more."

The boys had all been assigned to their Sirs. And only one portion of the initiation remained. Much like a college fraternity, a large Leather paddle came out of the supply closet. It would be the last opportunity for all the Club members to play with all the subs until training was over. The subs would be disciplined by their Sir, and by their Sir only. The boys in their Leather jockstraps were lined up and the Sirs took their best shots at the boys' handsome asses. The asses were blistered by the time all twelve Club members gave them as many whacks as they wished. The boys took their beatings proudly, because they were now the Leatherboys of the Gods of Leather Discipline.

With that the Leathermen celebrated, bringing out the five submissives who had been sequestered in another room. The Leathermen led their boys to the posts, slings, St. Andrew's crosses and workover tables. A fuckfest ensued. It lasted until dawn.

BONUS RAPE

Butch woke late the next morning. The new boy had been made to sleep on the floor, with chains holding him close to the bed frame.

Butch had slept in his Leathers- he enjoyed the sensuality of warmed Leathers caressing his body. He slept with Michael close to him.

Eventually, he would probably pull the other cop into bed too. But the trainee needed to be reminded of his submissive status and Butch enjoyed reminding a submissive of that status. He crawled out of bed and found the new boy still asleep. Michael was apparently downstairs as the aroma of morning coffee wafted upstairs.

Butch kicked the new boy with his booted foot.

"Up, boy."

The boy was slow in responding and so, he received another booted kick. The steel-toed boots had their effect and the boy jumped up with a yelp.

The boy stood facing Butch.

"First lesson of the day, boy, when your Sir says you get up, you fucking get up." Butch was right in the boy's face as he lectured him on his duties toward his Sir.

"Yes, Sir, thank you, Sir. I won't forget, Sir."

"Kneel, boy."

The boy obliged. Butch rubbed his swollen cock and then pulled off the cod. The cock was swollen with Butch's manpiss.

"Open your mouth, boy."

The boy obediently opened his mouth and Butch took a long and healthy piss down the boy's throat.

Butch unchained the boy from the bedframe, but placed a posture collar around the boy's neck. He attached a leash to the collar and led the boy downstairs.

"Good morning, Sir," Michael said as the two made their appearance in the kitchen, "Morning coffee is almost ready."

"Good, boy," Butch said, addressing Michael.

Michael knelt before his Master, who reached over and paddled his ass several times.

A voice on Michael's mobile unit broke the silence of the kitchen, "All units respond. All units respond immediately."

Michael looked in panic at Butch before rushing over to his uniform which had been torn off during afternoon sexplay the day before.

"This is Corrigan responding..." Michael said.

"Corrigan. Where are you?"

"About twenty minutes from headquarters, Sir."

"You got your gear?"

"Yeah, I've got my cycle here. I'm not scheduled for duty..."

"Need you. We've got a full-blown riot at the prison. Every available man is needed..."

"Yes, Sir. I'm on my way...."

Michael dressed hurriedly, checking to make sure his pistol was in his holster. He flew out the backdoor and down the backsteps. He checked to make sure he had his nightstick, pepper spray, and stun gun, before mounting up and tearing out of the driveway at breakneck speed.

Butch looked stunned. For the second time, he had just seen his boy react to a dangerous situation with quiet authority. "Damn," he thought, "this is the boy that I plant my cock up his ass and yet he could easily be a 'take charge' top. Damn, if I'm not lucky."

Butch turned on the television and it wasn't long before a special news report interrupted the usual morning crap.

The news reporter was reporting from the studio, "At 4:10 AM this morning, three Security Guards were stabbed and two were taken hostage by inmates at the Maximum Correctional Facility in an initial take-over. Apparently started by three inmates, several more inmates have joined the trio in releasing even more inmates who, in turn, have taken even more guards, some say as many as twenty, as hostages. State and local police units have been called into action." The newscast depicted a serene facility, but it was a stock photograph held by the news office.

Butch was distracted by the news. He was a caring man and worried about the safety of his boy. He thought momentarily about mounting up and going out to the prison, but dismissed that idea.

News flashes continued to interrupt the daily programming with the news becoming grimmer and grimmer with each new alert. As many as forty guards and prison personnel were in the prison, their status uncertain. A mobile unit from the news room was parked almost a mile away from the correctional facility. Obviously, no one was let inside except for police officers. A S.W.A.T. team was called in from the state capital but had not arrived as eleven o'clock rolled around.

Butch's phone rang. It was Max.
"You hear about the prison riot?"

"Yes. Yes, I did. Michael was called into duty."

"How about your other boy?"

In the excitement, Butch had forgotten that his other boy was a trained cop.

"Fuck, yeah, he could certainly help."

"I'm riding over… Snake and I will be there in a few…"

Meanwhile, the news reports kept coming in.

At 11:15, the reporter broke through the regular programming to update. "Two of the prisoners have escaped. They are considered armed and extremely dangerous. They apparently are the two who started the melee. They have been identified as Charles Scott Hopper, aged 42, 5 feet, 10-1/2 inches, 212 pounds, tattoos on his left shoulder and neck. Arrested recently for possession of cocaine with intent to distribute. Awaiting sentencing…." The voice droned on as Butch felt a sinking feeling in his stomach. He knew who the other escaped prisoner was without hearing any more. The reporter continued, "Franklin Edward Fortner, alias Frederick Edmund Lynch, aged 47…"

'Fuck em', Butch flatly stated.

"What, Sir?" the boy asked.

"Get suited up. We're gonna need your help." He slapped the boy sharply on his ass and demanded he dress in his uniform which had been discarded as soon as they had arrived back from the Club.

"Where's your gun, boy?"

"Back at the Club, I guess. They confiscated it when I was captured. What's up…?" the boy began. "Sir" he added.

"Those two escapees. Members of the Club put them where they were until this morning."

Butch made a hurried call to Carson and John. They had already heard the identifications and were suiting up.

"You stay the fuck where you are…," Butch yelled into the phone.

"No fucking way," Carson stated.

Butch argued but it was to no avail.

Snake and Max roared into Butch's driveway. The men were dressed in their heaviest cycle Leathers. Their saddlebags carried supplies for first aid and for torture.

Max roared into the house, not bothering to knock.

"You hear who the fuckers were? Those two sons-of-a-bitches. If they know what's good for them, they'll turn themselves in. I want to knock their fucking asses down. Hogtie them and fuck their god-damned asses." Max was furious and would not be quieted down. Butch tried to reason with him, but Max would not be convinced.

Snake was of a similar mind. In the meantime, the boy cop had returned downstairs, suited up in his uniform. His holster was empty.

Butch explained, "His gun was confiscated... you know where it is? We may need it for protection."

"So, you're in?" Snake questioned.

"If two of my Club brothers say we're in, we're in."

Snake confessed, "I have his gun- we took it away from him when we visited my dungeon. Thought it might be useful- it's out in my saddlebags along with some other necessary equipment."

Butch, having slept in his Leathers, was ready to ride so the three men and their cop submissive exited the house and mounted their cycles.

They headed to the area nearer the prison's grounds. Their testosterone was at a high level. Out on prowl. To capture two more boys. Bad boys. Bad fuckers. Nasty fuckers. Who needed to be punished.

Other members of the Club thought no differently. The guys had contacted one another so that no one rode alone.

They were out for high adventure.

They cruised through the streets and back alleys, dismounting to search abandoned sheds, unlocked garages.

Snake yelled something to Butch, but it was caught by the wind and Butch didn't hear what he said. Snake turned left and headed out of town. The guys had to do a turn-around to follow him. Snake had an intuitive mind, thinking, "What if they went to the same wooded area? It's an area that they have been to before- good place to hide." He wanted to search the area. It was a good thirty minutes away. He cranked up his cycle as he roared down the highway.

Max was contemplating what he would do to 'Fuck em' when, not if, he caught him. He wanted that bad ass all to himself. His old persona from 'Nam days surfaced. He thought about the buddies he had seen die a miserable death. He thought about the threats 'Fuck em' and Charlie had made to Phillippe and Carson.

Max was out for fucking revenge.

They idled down as they approached the wooded area. No sign of life, but the escaped convicts wouldn't be standing by the side of the road. Max jumped off his cycle and marched down the dirt path.

"All right, you scum-sucking son of a bitch," he bellowed, "it's Max. 'Mad' Max and I got a fucking score to settle with you, bro. You're a cowardly shithead. If you're hiding, come out like a man. Fucking coward."

The woods were silent. Rustling of leaves, bird song.

Max tore into the underbrush with his Leather brothers and the cop following him closely. The cop had retrieved his gun and had it poised.

They all peered into the woods, hoping to see a glimpse of the two men.

Suddenly, a crunching of underbrush came from immediately behind them. They all turned with fists raised and the gun pointed.

"Shit!" Max exclaimed. It was Carson, John and Phillippe. They had the same idea of where the convicts might have been hiding. The woods remained silent.

With a phalanx of other policemen, Michael was one of the policemen who entered the prison grounds. Yelling could be heard from inside the prison. Screams, cursing. Sheer chaos.

A unit of S.W.A.T. team members from the state capital had arrived and were suiting up for duty. Several units of cops were sent to guard the prisoners in the minimum and medium security units. They were on lock-down, of course, but the tension was palpable.

As a wedge, the first roster of policemen entered the building. Several guards were down- unconscious or possibly dead. The prison hallways looked like a war zone with furniture tossed around, apparently used as battering rams. Glass was shattered. Doors were broken off their hinges. Several cells hung ominously open.

Several wounded inmates were lying on the floor. A cop, who had served as a medic in Iraq, examined each one. Those with superficial wounds were locked in cells. Several more who required more serious attention were placed in one cell, with two guards standing outside. As the second wave of cops cautiously snaked through the building, Michael, who was among them, recognized 'Fuck em's cohort in one of the cells.

He had several deep gashes on his forehead.

Michael stopped and said, "So, they left you behind?"

The inmate looked up and spit at the cop.

Michael didn't react, simply continuing the taunting, "Yep, 'Fuck em' left you to dangle in the wind. This little escapade will get you life, you dumb bastard."

"Shut the fuck up. We'll get even with you. You're the fucking cop who turned us in. You and your faggot boyfriends."

Michael knew he had hit a pressure point and pursued it, "That's what 'Fuck em' considered you, his pussy boy. Left you behind and took Charlie with him. He isn't coming back for you, pussy boy."

The inmate lunged toward him, but of course, he was separated by a sturdy wall of concrete block. "He'll get even with your pussy friends. We found out where your queer ass Club meets..." The inmate suddenly shut up, realizing he had said too much.

Red flags went off in Michael's head.

"Shit," he thought, "I've got to get to the Club."

Without seeking permission from his commanding officer, he left the correctional facility and sped off on his motorcycle. Time was against him as he raced down the highway toward the Club.

The Leathermen searched the woods but there was no trace of the two escaped convicts.

"Wonder if anyone else has had any luck?" Carson said.

"Well, I have my cellphone and no one has called me," replied John.

He made several phone calls, but no one had any luck.

Michael arrived at the Club. There were no motorcycles parked nearby so he surmised that none of the Club members were there. However, the door possessed clear evidence that it had been tampered with. Michael tested the door knob and found that the door was unlocked. He pulled his gun from the holster as he cautiously entered.

His ears were sharply attuned to the silence of the interior. His ears strained to hear any noise that would indicate that the convicts were inside.

Minutes went by as he strained to hear any noise.

A voice broke the silence, "God damned it, Charlie, get your fucking ass in that sling. I need to fuck your ass."

"And I told you I ain't your fucking bitch. You can wait until one of those faggots comes marching back in here."

"I said, NOW! bitch" as a sharp slapping sound was heard.

"You fucking asshole!" as a scuffle was heard and grunts and groans as the two men continued to wrestle.

"I said...get in the... sling, bitch and I meant...it," 'Fuckem' said, as he continued to wrestle Charlie. Charlie was not going easily.

'Fuckem' finally succeeded in getting Charlie in the sling and handcuffing Charlie's hands to the suspension chains. There were pairs of handcuffs conveniently left there by the previous occupant.

'Fuckem' walked over to the supply cupboard and retrieved two ankle restraints. These were placed around Charlie's ankles, who was struggling in the sling. "Let me out of here, you fucking s.o.b.," Charlie said.

"As soon as I fist you and get my rocks off, bitch."

"You fucking asshole," Charlie said, as he struggled some more.

'Fuckem' marched back over to the supply closet and retrieved a bottle of lube. He greased up his hand and jammed it up Charlie's ass. Charlie let out a scream.

'Fuckem' slapped him and slapped him hard with a Leather paddle he had retrieved from the supply cupboard. He had clipped it to his orange jumpsuit pocket until ready for action.

He jammed his fist even harder into Charlie's fuckhole. Charlie screamed even more.

"What a pussy you are!" 'Fuckem' stated as he removed his fist and retrieved duct tape from the supply closet. He taped a piece squarely over Charlie's mouth and once again placed his fist in Charlie's hole.

Charlie's head was shaking violently from side to side. He was screaming vigorously but 'Fuckem' ignored his protests.

'Fuckem' withdrew his fist and greased up his cock. Against Charlie's muffled protests, 'Fuckem' rammed his meat up Charlie's aching hole.

'Fuckem' gripped Charlie's asscheeks and yelled "Fuck, boy, this feels great." He continued to pump. "You like a big convict pumping his pole in your hole?", 'Fuckem' said as he laughed sarcastically.

As he continued to pump his cock into Charlie's ass, 'Fuckem' suddenly felt the cold barrel of a gun against his left temple.

"Don't move a muscle or your cock won't be the only thing that discharges...," announced Michael as he quickly drew 'Fuckem's' hands behind his back and cuffed him. Michael anticipated the next action and caught his right leg between 'Fuckem's' leg, pressing sharply into the groin area. Michael escorted 'Fuckem' over to one of the St. Andrew's crosses and hogtied him around the waist to the cross. Kicking the convict's feet apart, he restrained the ankles to two points. It was then and only then that he released the handcuffs and re-cuffed the criminal's hands to the two remaining points of the cross. "Fuck em' was struggling and cursing at the cop the entire time, until Michael grabbed a discarded jockstrap from a nearby table and jammed it in the convict's mouth. Despite efforts to spit it out, 'Fuckem' failed.

'Fuckem' protested even more as Michael undressed him. He kicked and spit, cursed and threatened. 'But after all," Michael rationalized, "the orange jumpsuit is too distracting for the party I have in mind.... and I think the rest of the Club will agree." He was careful to uncuff only one appendage at a time, holding the gun close to 'Fuckem's temple as he pulled the jumpsuit off of him. Charlie protested less as his jumpsuit was removed, the fisting had apparently calmed him down considerably. The jumpsuits were stored in the supply closet- they would be needed for later. Michael hooded the two convicts. He added plugs in each one's mouth so that the surprise would not be spoiled by the guests of honor.

Michael pulled up a chair and eased himself into it. He kept his hand on his gun in case anything unexpected happened and settled in for the rest of the Club to return and find the final harvest.

The Club members had been in contact with each other with their cellphones. They agreed to rendezvous and re-strategize at the Club and twelve motorcycles roared back to their home base.

The men filtered in, finding Michael calmly sitting in a chair, facing two naked subjects- one manacled to the sling, one tied to the St. Andrew's Cross. Both hooded. The guys all questioned him, but Michael merely answered, "A bonus... wait 'til everyone gets here. If it pleases my Sirs"

Snake was one of the first to arrive. He went over to examine the captives. He recognized Charlie's tattoos but did not say anything to spoil Michael's feat. However, he would be first in line for any 'volunteer' activities.

When Carson entered, Michael rose from the chair and approached Carson. "Sir, we have two candidates who may be worthy of the Club's initiation."

"Well, son, we have a full complement of submissives. What makes these two so special?"

Michael filled him in.

When all the Club members arrived, Carson banged his fist on the makeshift podium.

"Men of Leather. A special evening- a boner's bonus, if you will. It seems that Michael, our newest Club member, has harvested two boys for a special added attraction. Michael has proven himself once again worthy of the Club by performing yet another valiant act of courage. The two boys that you see manacled to the St. Andrew's Cross and to the sling are pain pigs, fresh out of the correctional facility. Worthy of the Club's revenge."

Max rushed forward, yelling, "You mean he caught the sons of bitches? Fuck yeah. Let me at those holes- I want to stretch 'em to the next county."

Carson held him at bay (not an easy task), "Just a minute, Max. I'm exerting my Presidential powers. The one on the cross is all mine for the first go round." As Carson said this, he was rubbing his excited cock through his cod. It was soon hard and throbbing. Carson stood behind 'Fuckem' and that's exactly what he did. Thrusting his arched cock up 'Fuckem's' hole. 'Fuckem' thrashed and heaved but to no avail. Carson's cock had been waiting for this moment and prolonged it for a very long time, taunting 'Fuckem' during the rape of his innards.

Each Club member stepped up to the plate and before the night was through, Charlie and 'Fuckem' had each been sodomized a dozen times.

Michael added the lucky thirteen to the count. Ah, memories that last a life...sentence. Not only would they face the original charges. But adding to that... Inciting a riot. Wounding guards. Yeah, put away for a long time.

As Michael was placing his cock back in his cop's breeches, Butch placed his arm around his shoulder and said, "Hope you still want to be my boy." Butch looked at him with hopeful eyes.

"Yes, Sir," was Michael's reply.

"Let's get these scumbags back to where they belong." Carson ordered.

The prisoners were taken out of their manacles but there was no spirit left in them. They were redressed in their orange jumpsuits, tied tightly with bondage rope, manacled to two of the cycles, and dumped outside the prison gates. The riot was apparently at an end, the compound looked tranquil in the early dawn light. Guards reporting for the 0600 hours shift found the two escapees expertly tied into two neat bundles, lying right outside the prison gates.

The Gods of Leather Discipline Club continues to flourish. Two new members have been accepted into the Club. A full complement of submissives serve the Leathermen of the Club. The two new members are in need of good boys, however. And several of the Club members have decided they would like a second boy for their personal pleasuring. And so, harvest time is soon to commence. A harvest of G.O.L.D..

ABOUT THE AUTHOR

G.W. Leatherman Parks has been a Leatherman for over thirty years. He is a proud member of the Leather Archives and Museum in Chicago and writes frequently for FLAGSHIP, the newsletter of Fits Like a Glove. He has also been published in *Drummer and Cuir: For LeatherMen by LeatherMen*. He is a collector of vintage Leather, Leather artwork and photography.

This is G.W. Leatherman Parks' third book. His first book *Leatherdaddy* and second book *Leather Nazis* are available from Amazon.com, TheNazcaPlainsCorp.com or your local bookstore.

LEATHERDADDY

Erotic Literature by the Black Leather Gloved Hands of

G.W. LEATHERMAN PARKS

A BONER BOOK

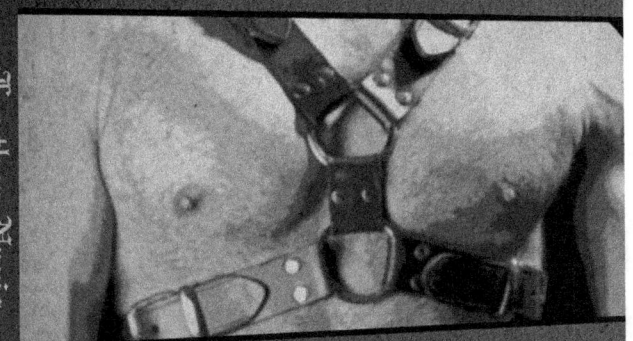

Leather Nazis

Erotic Literature by
the Black Leather Gloved Hands of

G.W. Leatherman Parks

A
Boner
Book

www.ingramcontent.com/pod-product-compliance
Lightning Source LLC
Chambersburg PA
CBHW051145260626
47170CB00005B/1962